The Woman *in the* Woods

EASTERN WASHINGTON UNIVERSITY PRESS

The Woman *in the* Woods

LINKED STORIES

Ann Joslin Williams

12 11 10 09 08 07 06 5 4 3 2 1

Cover and interior design by A. E. Grey
Cover illustration: Lance W. Clayton, "A Woman Hugging a Tree"

Library of Congress Cataloging-in-Publication Data

Williams, Ann Joslin.
The woman in the woods : linked stories / Ann Joslin Williams.
p. cm.
ISBN 1-59766-019-1
I. Title
PS3623.I556293W66 2006
813'.6—dc22
2006020081

The paper used in this publication meets the minimum requirements of ANSI/NISO Z39.48-1992 (Permanence of Paper).

EASTERN WASHINGTON UNIVERSITY PRESS
Spokane and Cheney, Washington

For my mother,

and in memory of my father,

Thomas Williams

Contents

Acknowledgments

I WANT TO THANK the Wallace Stegner Program at Stanford University, the Iowa Writers' Workshop, and the University of New Hampshire for support while writing these stories. I am incredibly grateful to all the people over the years who've read these stories and offered editorial advice and encouragement, especially Gregory Spatz for his generous counsel on everything I have ever written since we were students at UNH a very long time ago. Infinite thanks to brilliant writers and bighearted readers Daniel Orozco, Doug Dorst, Andrea Bewick, Malinda McCollum, Eliza Harding, Debbie Hodge, and Karen Dufour. I'm indebted to Lois Rosenthal and Robley Wilson for publishing my first stories. With great appreciation, thanks to Dorian Karchmar. Huge thanks go to my inspiring teachers: John Yount, Mark Smith, Joseph Monninger, Frank Conroy, James Alan McPherson, Marilynne Robinson, Judith Grossman, Tobias Wolfe, John L'Heureux, Gilbert Sorrentino, Elizabeth Tallent, and my father, Thomas Williams. With immense gratitude and for always believing in me, thanks to Pete and Tamara, Art and Celeste, Ted and Janet, Bill Morrissey, and the Tea Party women. Above all, thanks to my mother, Elizabeth Blood Williams, for just about everything in the world.

The names of the trees are still known in Leah.
In the fall the deer are the color of the spaces between the trees.

—Thomas Williams, *Leah, New Hampshire*

By some chance, here they are, all on this earth; and who shall ever tell the sorrow of being on this earth, lying on quilts, on the grass in a summer evening, among the sounds of the night.

—James Agee, *A Death in the Family*

Cold-Fire

THE CABIN WHERE I LIVE, the one my parents built when they were young and strong and fearless, sits on a hill overlooking the valley in front of Mount Cascom. Mount Cascom is 3,121 feet. A medium-sized mountain for New Hampshire. It's bald on top, sheer granite, rich with glittering mica. Ribbons of white quartz fold into clefts and make you think of snow drifts, though it's summer. From my front porch the fire tower on the summit looks like a tiny spaceship, set down atop the dome.

The fire watchman's name is Gordon. He's a tall man with a long white braid that swings over his rucksack as he strides down the hill those mornings after he's stayed here with me. Though I hate to see him leave, it's nice to know he'll be up there in the tower, keeping watch.

Gordon is fifty-four, fourteen years older than I am. Except for the color of his hair, I wouldn't have guessed him over fifty; his job keeps him fit. His arms are hard cords of muscle, though not thick or heavy; it's as if they have been shaped from straining against hundreds of years of weather. At tree line there are dwarf spruce—their trunks gracefully knurled and scrolled, forever suffering the wind.

Gordon's quarters are off summit. I stayed there only once. It was cramped. He sleeps in a single bed. At night the wind wails like ghosts rushing in a fury through the spruce, scraping painfully around the edges of his cabin. Gordon talks in his sleep. Once I heard my name. And then another word which could have been *marry*, or *merry*, or *Mary*.

At dusk I sit on my porch. The silhouette of the ridges makes a giant woman lying on her back. He never comes when I'm longing for him; it's only when I'm busy, not thinking—then there he'll be, hiking out of the woods in his heavy boots.

I remind myself: Don't imagine anything that hasn't happened yet. Don't think about the past. Stay in the space between *then* and *what's-to-come*—it's the only relief.

I'll just say this once, then I won't return to it: My son died when he was four years old. He stepped off the roof with his umbrella and his imagination, but neither kept him in the air. We have long since sold that house with that roof.

I lose track of my husband, Thomas, and his many destinations; he's trying to outrun grief. He's phoned from Montana, Washington, Mexico. More recently, a postcard from Vietnam, land of his birth, and where he has a mother he's never met. Do I miss him? What I miss is the impossible—all of us alive and happy and moving into our abruptly ended future. So, there's no point in dwelling on it. Though hope can still get her hands on me, gripping and greedy.

There's always work to be done—brush to be cut, chimney to be cleaned, knives to be sharpened, carpenter ants to be exterminated, garden to be weeded. I can stay busy all day long. At night, that's when it's hard. Sometimes I bake—sifting, beating, kneading. But I'm usually baking for Gordon—a form of longing. Sometimes, though, I bake for Bella, the old woman who is my nearest neighbor. Gordon calls her Blowsabella because her hair is a huge mess of tangles as if it's been blown crazy by the wind, snagged by branches and angry birds. I'm sure you couldn't get your fingers through it if you tried. She has a grin full of gaps and gold that can turn an astray tramper's skin to goose pimples.

Now, I slide pans into the oven, thinking about her remedy for keeping slugs out of my garden; I'm pondering what containers to use. Then, behold! Here he comes.

I'm here because there's no one else to take care of this place. My brother, David, lives in Colorado with his wife and three children. He sends money to help pay the taxes. He can't do more; he and Anna have happily settled out West; he is a college professor, she is a botanist. My mother passed last year, my father when I was a girl. I can't sell the cabin. They pitched a tent by the brook, skinned logs, mixed cement, hauled rocks. At the end of the day they sat on the roof beams and watched stars surface above the mountain. I can't let it go.

Gordon is here. He breathes in the warm air of my kitchen. "It's heaven," he says.

"It's pie," I tell him. "Peach."

Later, I put one pie away for Bella, and take the other to the front porch where we eat with forks, right out of the pan.

Between bites, he asks how my day was.

"I worked my butt off clearing brush," I say.

"Don't do that," he says. "I'd hate to see anything happen to it."

It's been a long time since I've been admired. In bed Gordon pushes me over on my back and throws the sheet off.

Then his eyes rove over me, up and down; he follows where he's looking with his fingers. He slides his fingers between my legs.

Fire watchmen don't look for fire. They look for smoke. Smoke curling up out of the green rolling hills, out of the junipers and scrub at the base of the ledges, and the clearings where there are remote buildings such as mine and Bella's.

None of us stays here year round. The roads can be impassable in snow. In the winter Gordon will work as a night security guard for an office complex in Canaan, on the other side of the mountain. I'll work for a newspaper, and live on the other side of the state. I do not want to think about this.

Gordon's expressions can be hard to read—his features aren't exactly symmetrical. A while back, he stood me naked in front of the mirror, looked over my shoulder. "Can't you see what I see?" he said. Though he seemed to be smiling, his voice was stern. "No, don't look at me," he said. "There."

Bella bathes in the brook where there's a deep pool. She takes her clothes off and walks right into the freezing water up to her thighs. With a cake of biodegradable soap she suds up from head to knee, then drops below the surface in a quick dunk to rinse off. If a tramper stumbles upon this little known spot, he might see an old woman shooting out of the water, breasts flopping, paunch jiggling, gobs of dripping hair stuck to her face and hanging to her middle. Soap suds drifting away from bowed, craggy legs. And then her eye-biting stare, the grin opening across her face, her hand squeezing a breast as if to mock him before he cuts and runs.

I bring Bella bread and casseroles and sweets. She trades me with advice about maintenance, and tells me stories. In

1921 the mountain burned. Lightning struck a tree and set it on fire. The fire bloomed and hopped incredible distances, fueled by wind and dry wood from a dry summer, and the unexplainable behavior of fire. The flames spun into a huge funnel, which twisted along the ridge, eating everything. Once it was done there were no trees to hold the soil and that's why the summit is exposed.

The first time I saw Gordon was at the beginning of the summer. He was by the brook, lying on his belly across a boulder, sleeves pushed up, arms hanging over the edge, fingers spread. I came upon him unexpectedly. I don't see people in the woods often, especially not at my stream, my rock. I stayed downwind of him as if he were a bear and might smell me. I thought I smelled him. Sweat and wet wool, but also something sweet, like maple sap, boiling off.

He'd tucked his braid into his collar; later it would surprise me to see how long it was. I crouched low and glared at him; this was my place, and I had intended to nap in the sun. The brook was full from three days of rain, and spun around rocks, creating little eddies and catches of white foam. I could not believe anyone could stay still so long. It was as if he were made of stone.

The side of Gordon's mouth is paralyzed so in one corner his lips tuck together as if they've been sewn shut.

"You make me dansey-headed," he says, and rolls onto his back. We have just made love.

Even though I've never heard this expression, I say, "At least I know you're not talking out of both sides of your mouth."

He smiles, one side happy, one side grieved. His face is on the fence. If you manage to blur his features, you get mischief, you get the devil in him. It's the face of the fire watchman, setting me on fire. Burning me up.

"Maybe," I say, "your mother never turned you as a baby. Maybe the dryads forgot to rip out all the stitches. Maybe you slept on ice for too many years. Good thing I'm here to warm you up."

"You are young," Gordon whispers close to my ear. His voice is like flour sifting through my fingers, soft and cool. "Why are you hiding out here on this mountain? You should be married. You should have a passel of children loving you."

An ache rolls my heart over. There are things he doesn't know.

"I can't let it go to the weeds," I tell him. "The wilderness is licking its chops."

Gordon has spotted smoke in distant valleys and reported it. Though lightning is the most common, fires are often started by people: campfires left smoldering, cigarettes tossed carelessly. Since 1921 there haven't been any forest fires on Mount Cascom. There was talk once of closing the tower. The state wanted to save money, cut the watchman's job, but it didn't happen. It's a popular mountain. There are good views. Hikers flock to the campground in Canaan. With binoculars I can see people on the top walking around below the steel girders of the tower. They look like tiny iron filings, magnetic, upright.

Gordon keeps the hatch closed when he's up there. He doesn't like hikers climbing the metal stairs, poking their heads through the floor, squinting through his telescopes, leaving fingerprints on the glass protecting his geodetic map, pointing to mountains in the distance and naming them wrong.

I never care to go up into the tower; I went there plenty as a girl. Now, when I climb the mountain, I sit off to the side, away from people milling about, and look out at the valley, at all the greens. The dark olive greens of white pine, black spruce, hemlock, balsam, junipers. The brilliant yellow-greens of birch, beech, maple, poplar.

In late June, Gordon watched a woman from his tower, making her way up the granite. He was curious because, unlike other hikers, she didn't come all the way to the top. She didn't carry a pack, no water, no sweater, no lunch, no binoculars, no map. He lowered his telescope and tried to see her face through wildly blowing hair. She reached back, gathered it around her hand—*hair the color of golden wheat*—as if to let him catch a glimpse. Then she let it go, but not before he saw in her face what he calls a *cold-fire*—a fire laid, but unlit. He said he was inexplicably drawn to me.

I'd never seen anyone catch a fish with his bare hands. I heard him grunt and there was a splash, and then a trout came sailing over the scrub and landed at my feet. The fish flopped and twisted, instinctively trying to hurdle itself back toward the brook. Then another came flip-falling from the sky, slapping through the leaves and branches, whipping to and fro. The next nearly hit me on the arm. It was raining brookies.

The morning after that I went to see Bella. She was behind her house, whacking the ground with a hoe. The soil was hard and dry and didn't give easily, but she'd managed two long rows of upturned dirt.

"What are you going to plant there?" I asked.

"Weed," she said angrily, as if she knew it was impossible to grow anything there. Then I realized she meant marijuana.

"What do you know about the new fire watchman," I asked. She didn't say anything. "I brought cake," I said, remembering, and held out a tinfoil-wrapped package. "I saw him catch trout with his hands."

She grinned to herself. That grin that scares most people, her cheeks scrunching into a thousand rubbery folds.

"What kind of cake?" she said, finally, eager as a little girl.

"Carrot. With cream cheese frosting."

She nodded, pleased, then swung her hoe for another wedge. She said, "He asked me to cook his fish once."

"Did you?"

Bella gave me a look like I'd just suggested we take a rocket to the moon.

Bella calls me a weatherspy because I watch the sky most every night. It's a habit of mine since I was a girl; my parents, my brother, and I would climb the ladder to the roof to catch the Perseids.

It was there, when I was stretched out on the still-warm shingles, that I heard him come to my cabin below. I heard his wet boots squeak across the porch, the spring on the screen door chirp. Heat went through me. How dare he enter my house! How dare he clomp his soggy boots into my kitchen? And then a chill when I heard him take hold of the ladder, bounce it against the eave, and begin to climb. I hid behind the chimney, pressed to the cool stones. He stopped at the top of the ladder.

"Are you up here?" he asked.

His voice took me by surprise. It wasn't gruff as I'd imagined it to be, but soothing as a hush.

"Girl?" he said. No one had called me girl for years. "I'm starved. Belly-pinched. I know you bring cake to that disagreeable old woman." He chuckled, then said in a softer tone, "I saw you, by the way."

I knew he meant at the brook. I'd sneaked off when he finished throwing fish my way.

"Take whatever you want," I said.

He laughed, then swung himself atop. I felt uneasy; he was a big man, and I didn't know his temperament. He walked past me, up the slant of the shed roof to the high eave where he sat down, dangled his legs off and leaned back on his palms. It made me queasy to see him that close to the edge.

"Did I say you could come up here?" I peeked around the chimney. He was only a silhouette, except for his glowing braid that I now saw hung halfway down his back.

"I come in peace," he said, then laughed.

"You smell," I said, for in that instant an unpleasant waft of fish odor came my way.

He was silent for a bit, then said, "I'm sorry for that." He sounded truly ashamed. I almost apologized, but he rose and went down the ladder, and the hill, until I couldn't hear his footfalls anymore.

Two nights later I was in the kitchen cleaning up when he knocked on my screen door, and walked in as if he were welcome.

"Have I missed dessert?" he said.

I squinted at him. I didn't want to be taken advantage of. But I had unfrosted meringue left over from a Jerusalem pudding cake I'd brought to Bella. His eyes had found it already. It sat lopsided under a clear plastic cover.

"I have always had a yearning for sweets," he admitted as if it were a bad thing. And then his eyes fell on my chest, and slid away. I thought I saw a look of shame come over him, pulling his mouth down—on the one side. Or maybe it was pity. I am forty, small breasted and thin in that drained way when weight has come off too quickly. I can smooth the flesh around my jaw to see the suggestion of a younger face. My smile has worn out, my eyes are weary. The curves of my figure are unwilling. Four years of grieving must show through my skin like a skeleton. This is how I thought he saw me that night.

"You probably never saw anyone guddle fish," he said, proudly, raising a paw and making a quick grasp at the air.

"It takes patience," he said. "Convince them you're part of the landscape. Find a whirlpool that keeps up a froth. Trout can't see through it."

I remembered that the brook was running fast that day, stirring up foam, keeping Gordon hidden from the trout. But then I wondered about it the other way around—weren't the trout hidden as well?—and this is something I've never understood.

He ate with a fork, smashing the meringue into the tines and licking the fork twice for every mouthful, turning it over and back. He made noises of pleasure, then set the fork down and squashed up the crumbs with his finger, licked them off. When he was done he pushed away from the table.

"Thank you, Kate," he said. Then he was gone, leaving behind smells of wet earth, moss-covered granite, and something softer, like the mint of freshly cut birch. I hadn't heard my name in a man's mouth in a long time.

∞∞∞∞∞

Bella is arthritic, but she manages. She smokes pot for the pain. Besides canned food and my offerings, she grows vegetables. Her garden is overrun with witch grass and chickweed, but still it produces more than enough. Paper cups full of pee sit strategically at the corners of her garden; animals don't like the smell of human urine. Though groundhogs are another story. They're harder to deter. Sometimes she lies on the roof of her cabin with a .22, waiting for her opportunity.

The other day I watched yellow jackets feed on a ball of hamburger Bella had hung from a tree in a mesh of wire to lure them. They'd been bothering her, dithering in her space, alighting on the rim of her glass of beer. She'd placed a bucket of water under the bait. The yellow jackets gorged themselves until they were too heavy, dropped and drowned.

In the fall a grandson will come and take Bella to New York City where I imagine she's just as eccentric as she is here on the mountain, only perhaps a bit cleaner, dressed more heavily for the cold weather, and unarmed.

Like me, she's reluctant to leave. She loves the deep woods—the every-which-way of branches overhead. The sound of the brook, constant in her ears just outside her windows. Like me, she loves the solitude. But sometimes I look at her and worry. Will I be her one day? Old and alone. Face of a dried apple?

The third time Gordon came to my cabin we made love. His mouth tasted of smoke and wintergreen. He pushed me against the kitchen wall and kissed me for a long time. Then his hands moved over my breasts, and down, finding buttons. He undressed me between kisses. When he felt how wet I was, he sighed like he'd just found a treasure. He said, "You are so beautiful." He pressed his fingers deep inside me, lifted me a little. I was barely able to breathe. I wanted him to grip me, take all he wanted.

"I am *here*," I said, more to myself than him.

"I am too," he said.

Sometimes I think about winterizing the cabin. Gordon and I could live here year round. We could be like two bears in a cave. Hibernate. Only go out occasionally for supplies.

Stop, I tell myself. The future is only a fantasy.

Fourth of July and Gordon and I are on top of the mountain. From here we can see fireworks going off in all the distant towns. It's like watching whales spout sparks out of a black sea. We sit out on the ledge. Blowsabella, Gordon announces, has generously donated some of her homegrown in celebration of Independence Day, so we smoke a little.

Stars are within reaching distance. I put my hand up and swat them. Gordon slides his around with a finger, like moving silver coins on a surface, and forms a new constellation.

"This is Kate's constellation," he says, drawing an outline.

"God should have thought of that," I say. "A heart-shaped constellation. What's with all these dippers anyway?"

The wind picks up, making our perch uncomfortable. We start the trek from tower to timberline. The granite is steep; I have to go slow, making sure the treads of my sneakers hold. Gordon gets ahead of me, and soon, I can't make out his shape. Though I'm still inching along, rock under my feet, I have the feeling that I'm scaling the dark wall of the sky. I am walking my way down the shell of the stratosphere, following the curve of the globe. Below is a black ocean, full of fire-spouting creatures and drowning yellow stars. My lover has vanished. My husband, my parents. My son. I lift my arms to fly.

Next, I smell maple and mildew. Gordon is carrying me to his bed.

That night ghosts scrape around the corners of his cabin. I never sleep there again.

In late July the freezer is packed with jars of pesto and tubs of blueberries. The garden is done with snap peas and most of the greens, but now brimming with zucchini, carrots, cucumbers, and beets. The soup bowls I'd filled with beer to draw the slugs are full of rainwater and dirt. I pour them out, take them in.

Five nights go by and Gordon doesn't come. I tromp on the roof. Pace around the chimney. Where is he? A tree uprooted and pinned him somewhere deep in the forest. Lightning found its tallest point—a man on a ledge. There's someone named Mary in Canaan. No, I calm myself. No.

I bake for Bella. Angel food cake with vanilla frosting—her favorite. Ginger cookies because she craves them. Blueberry muffins, she asked for them.

And then, yes! He is coming through the door.

I don't ask him the reason for being gone so long because I don't want to find out anything that might blacken our days together. I run my fingertips across the grain of his ribs. He breathes half words, nonsense sounds that drop from his lips in his sleep. I think of my mother, lying in this very bed so many years without her husband. *I can't imagine my life,* she told me once, *if I hadn't had you and David.*

I will never have another child.

ooooooooooo

Earlier in the summer, Gordon stood me naked in front of the mirror.

"You," he told the image in the mirror. "A beautiful, sexy woman."

I looked away.

"No, don't look at me," he said. "There."

I turned my eyes on myself reluctantly. It was not my own gaze, but Gordon's that opened me. How do you explain it? It's unexplainable. Bella noticed, said I was glowing. I could have sprinted up the mountain. Caught the heels of hikers, leapt over them.

The first week in August Gordon agrees to accompany me to town for breakfast. Every other week I go in for the mail, and groceries; this is the first time he's ever come with me. I glance around the crowded diner. I am a person like any other. Eggs. Bacon. Not even Gordon's uniform or long white hair seem to garner any notice. We share a newspaper. I start to feel queasy; the words blur. Too much grease? Then it passes.

There's an article in the paper about a logger who was trapped under a tree.

"'Man amputates own leg to save himself,'" I read aloud. "Idaho. That's peculiar," I say. "Remember, Gordon? There was that man in Pennsylvania just last week? The guy whose tractor tipped over on him?"

I'd heard it on the radio. He'd lain in his back-forty for two days before he'd freed himself by taking a pocket knife to his leg just below the knee.

"And I swear," I say, remembering, "there was another last month somewhere in Oklahoma—a man trapped under his car—did the same."

Gordon reaches for his coffee, takes a side-mouth sip. Puts the cup back in the saucer.

"It seems to be happening all over the country," he says.

I start to laugh, and then more, harder, until my stomach feels like rock. A little boy a few tables over catches sight of me and laughs too. I can feel how wide my mouth is. Gordon is laughing a little, but then he starts to look concerned, brows arched. I'm laughing, but it could seem like crying. I cover my mouth. The laughing isn't laughing anymore. Merry tripped sorry, Bella would say. Why am I crying?

The smaller summit next to Cascom is called Firescrew because of the spiral of fire that rolled itself along the curve of the valley. Firescrew is also barren, though long ago it was covered with tracts of pasture—golden wheat that grew between stone walls and ancient deciduous trees. If Cascom is the breast, then Firescrew is the swollen belly.

At night the air gets cool and we contemplate building a fire in Bella's fireplace. We are here with fried trout, lightly breaded and browned to perfection; green beans steamed and doused with butter, sprinkled with almond slivers; linguini covered with creamy green pesto; a bottle of dry white wine. Since Bella's chimney hasn't been cleaned for God knows how many years, we decide against it and make do with sweaters and kerosene lanterns.

We eat at Bella's long dining room table. So many chairs, as if she has grand dinner parties with people we don't know about. She smiles like a queen as we fill her plate, serving her.

I sip wine, watch my people. Gordon, younger in the lantern light, and laughing. Bella talking, telling us stories about misguided hikers—two who thought her house was a public lodge, walked right in and sat on her couch, until she climbed from the roof, .22 in hand.

Gordon says, "You're giving me a cramp, Blowsabella." She punches him in the arm, but she likes the name; she's heard it from him before.

I have to pee again. Bella eyes me as I leave the room. My body is unfamiliar. But I don't want to think about this.

When I come back Bella has unearthed a guitar. She holds it toward me and says, "Sing for us, Kate."

I shake my head. I don't sing anymore; she knows this. And besides the guitar has only five strings and looks like it's been used as a river paddle.

"I beg you," Gordon says.

"No," I say firmly so they'll stop. Bella nods and takes the guitar to the other room. I'm relieved to see it go.

Gordon takes my hand, pulls me to his side. "Will I ever hear your voice?"

"This is it," I say.

Bella surprises us with a pan of brownies for dessert. One half regular, one half pot. Without asking, she drops a regular one from her spatula onto my plate. Gordon chooses his own brownie, regular too. Bella eats three pot brownies before we are saying goodnight, turning on our flashlights and following the trail back to my cabin.

"I'm worried," I tell Gordon.

"She's all right," he says, mistaken about what I intended to say.

Late August: A letter from Thomas. He's located his mother. She doesn't speak English, and he speaks only a little

Vietnamese. Still, they manage to communicate. She gave him up because his father was a missing American soldier; "half-and-half" babies were outcasts. Missionaries took Thomas to America to be adopted. She put her hand on her breast to show him how it pained her to let him go. He has three sisters—half, that is. At the end he writes: *I miss you, Kate.* When I read these words my heart splits, one part turns back.

Bella smokes the last of last year's stash. She sits on her front stoop, holding a match over the filled pipe, sucking the flame down.

Her knuckles are knobby with arthritis. I don't know how she can bend them. She looks thinner to me; the collar of her sweater hangs low, revealing a skinny, plaited neck. She tokes on the pipe, squints with one eye through the smoke.

"Near September," she says, and I know she means that summer is coming to an end and soon her grandson will come fetch her.

I put a bag of muffins on the stoop next to her. She nods at the bag, grins around her pipe.

"What are you going to do?" she asks.

"About what?"

She gives me a look like I just asked the pope what he thought about abortion.

The mountain is already changing colors. Dabs of red bloom amid the greens. The garden has produced cabbage, broccoli, more tomatoes than anyone can eat. The brambles at the edge of my field are heavy with fat blackberries, threatening to drop at any time.

"I have in mind a blackberry pie," I tell Gordon.

"My darling," he says. He lies next to me on the roof. "What will I do without you?"

"Why should you be without me?" I put my fingers on his lips, afraid of what he'll say.

"That's funny," he says. He presses his own fingers against the corner of his mouth.

"Gordon," I ask. "Would you cut off your leg if you were trapped, pinned, say, under a tree, and you knew that no one would ever find you?"

Gordon is still testing his lip. He reaches for my finger and uses it to poke himself. "I'll be the devil," he says. "I'm feeling this."

I stretch, yawn. "That's because I've decided to turn you into a human being."

"You are a stitch," he says. Then he answers my question: "I believe I would."

That night I dream of a great fire. It roars down the mountain, pauses at the brook, sways madly; then, as if it's summoned its twin, the opposite bank ignites. Trees explode. The fire rushes up the valley toward my cabin. From a distance I see Bella and Gordon twirl like witches, hair flying out, urging it on. The fire springs onto my roof, engulfs it, burns the place down to its stones.

And then . . . I am free.

When I wake up I feel sick and guilty. Gordon breathes next to me in the dark.

"Gordon?" I whisper. He doesn't stir. "I had a bad dream."

I hear an owl, its haunting call—three staccato notes, one long, guttural. Another owl echoes the first, farther away.

Gordon's hair is a cobweb across the pillow. His arms lie slack on top of the sheet. In this non-light, it seems as if I'm sleeping with a very old man.

On Labor Day Bella's grandson comes to take her back to New York City. Before she goes she gives me a jar of carrot marmalade, a flask of blackberry cordial, and a baggie of pot for Gordon. Her grandson turns off the pump, drains the pipes, yanks the circuit breaker, locks her doors. Bella moves slower, talks less. It's as though she ages instantly at his arrival. The grandson has his one duty—to retrieve his grandmother and bring her back to civilization. He's pleasant enough, tolerant, patient. He cringes, then laughs when I tell him what's in the paper cups around her garden.

Before he helps Bella into his jeep, I stand in front of her. I want to kiss her. I've never touched her, much less kissed her. It seems impossible to do it, but I must. And then I do. Her cheek is supple, and soft; my lips stick a little. She's startled, maybe embarrassed, but when I pull back I see her eyes full of water, and her grin breaking out, almost pretty. Then she waves me off and takes her grandson's hand. My nose tingles, but I won't cry in front of them.

"Go home," Bella says.

I have the feeling she doesn't mean my cabin, but I say, "I am home."

Bella gives me a look like she wasn't born yesterday.

Soon Gordon is leaving too.

"No," I say. "No, you can't leave." We stand in front of my fireplace, though we haven't lit the touchwood—not cold enough yet.

I laugh because we are kidding; it's not really goodbye—we'll return weekends through the fall. But this is when the other worry is creeping up. This is when I finally hear the words in my head: *Are you pregnant?* If true, no point in telling; I'll never have it. Then: *Joy, joy, joy. You want this!* No. I do not. Besides, it's impossible; Gordon has been sterile for years. *Haven't you been sick and having to pee all the time?* Stop.

"Please stay." I tug his sleeves, teasing him. "What will I do without you?"

"I really do have to go," he says, but a little too seriously.

An ancient fear passes through me.

"No," I whisper. "Everyone leaves."

Everyone leaves.

And then I do too.

The thing about the future is that it does come, and instantly is not the future anymore, and so you look forward again, making the fantasy, the one you hope for.

I didn't return to the mountain until the first weekend in October. The air was frozen. I built a roaring fire, roasted one side, then the other, until the room was warm enough so I could move away. There was the lookout tower, bright, sparkling. I didn't think about him.

I didn't. But wouldn't he see the smoke from my chimney? Wouldn't he come?

It took me so long to come back partly because of Thomas. More letters came with more details of his new family. Photographs: smiling Vietnamese faces surrounding his own Vietnamese face. He looked good, healthy, young.

I was paralyzed. My period was three weeks late. I lay on my back and ran my hands over my breasts, my swollen belly. I couldn't make myself find out for sure. It seemed safer to remain in a state of suspension. I thought of my mother, running her hand over her breast, discovering the strange, hard pit growing deep under the surface, fingers sliding away, the choice to persuade herself it wasn't there.

I wrote reviews and worked late at the newspaper. Then, my period came. I couldn't believe it. Amazing. My body had been fooled by its own desires. How convincing it was. I was stunned.

No decision to make after all. No fate laid in my lap. No child to fetch me back to civilization.

I laughed into the mirror, until it wasn't laughing anymore. Where was the little girl who was going to grow up and live on the mountain just as her parents did? Where was the woman who married Thomas with her heart practically jumping out of her mouth? And the mother who tumbled softly in love with her son? Where was the girl who once sang songs with her father? Where was she if she wasn't me?

I think of Gordon, looking out his windows, watching the woman make her way up the granite. This time she doesn't stop short of the tower. If she glances toward the windows she won't see him because he has moved back, busy with a radio call, making sure it's nothing important.

I reach the metal stairs, surprised to see the hatch is open above. I feel a flutter-tug in my belly—a little fish whipping its tail? I wonder if this is what it's like to lose a limb and still feel as if it's there.

Then my head is through, and I see boots and the green pant legs of his uniform. My heart is booming. I come all the way, hoist myself up by the rail and stand.

A man looks at me. "Nice day, isn't it?" he says.

I look around the small space for another face. There are the windows, the mountains in the distance.

"I thought Gordon," I say. I can barely get enough air.

This new watchman is young, husky, like a Marine—all buttoned collar and crew cut.

"The watchman," I say.

It takes him a moment, then he nods, remembering. "Gone. Went south somewheres, I think."

"South? He'll be back?"

"Not as far as I know. I'm stationed here permanent. He retired. Had family, or his wife's family in Texas, I think it was.

"You okay, Ma'am?" He takes two quick steps forward, but I have gripped the rail.

The woman takes a different trail down. It's a sharp descent over sheer granite, until the trail hits a straightaway through dwarf spruce, and meanders along the easy ridge to Firescrew. Up close, the white braids of quartz woven into the granite are tinged with rust-colored veins. The plateau has more growth than she remembered. Yellow grasses, fine and tall with delicate feathery seeds; junipers and low blueberry bushes everywhere.

I cross the height-of-land, then down the mountain under the new hardwoods, still holding fast to their fire-lit leaves.

Before This Day There Were Many Days

THEY HEARD THEIR MOTHER YELL their father's name, and came from their beds barefoot and squinting. Jeff Driver was in the kitchen. He was crying, and he told them that the bridge on Cascom Mountain Road had washed out. He looked at Kate's mother and said her name, "Carey." Then he looked at Kate and David, and no one spoke. The floor was tracked with water and cold under Kate's feet. The front door was open and it was raining hard.

"Down to Lorde's place," Jeff said. "The truck just went over. Swept off."

Their mother lifted her arms as if she didn't dare touch herself, or close up and only find emptiness. Her hair was dripping.

Kate pressed against David's arm. Then David hit Jeff, swung out and punched him in the shoulder and Jeff hung his head, and put his hand on the spot where David had struck him. Their mother said to stop and there was the water drumming and pouring from the gutters, and suddenly it all went still, like that, and Kate heard the words as if they were said right next to her ear: "He's dead."

ooooooooo

Before their mother yelled *Lendel* into the night, they'd been in their rooms and Kate had been asleep. Before that, she was awake. It wasn't raining then. It was hot, sticky. She searched for the cool spots with her feet, and every now and then she snapped the top sheet up like a parachute and let it fall slowly and coolly back on her body. The crickets trilled in the field, and far down in the valley she heard the brook. The noise of the brook was constant, a muffled roar, a rushing sound, but louder than usual. It was overflowing, full of all the rain of the past few weeks. She and David had been down there. Fast water tore up the banks and dragged down bushes and little trees, and there was foam and swirling pools, all that water in such a hurry. It was remarkable to think the rain had done this. The sound was so loud that you had to shout to be heard, so she and David hadn't said much. They stood and watched, then ran along the bank upstream. There was a big rock they knew of that rose above a pool. It was a broad expanse of granite that stretched across the brook like the smooth back of a whale. You could fit your body into its potholes and worn spots. It felt soft, almost. Now the rock was completely underwater, and you wouldn't know it was there except for a dip in the surface where a rill folded backwards. Also how the water streaming over the top took the rock's shape, only glassy and moving. The beaver lodge was gone, washed away. The beaver dam too, completely knocked out, but there were still some of their felled trees caught up on the side, the ends chewed into sharp points.

From her bed she could forget it was the sound of the brook just as you forget the hum of a refrigerator until it clicks off. The grown-ups were on the front porch. There was her mother and father and Jeff Driver. They were drinking cool drinks; she could hear ice cubes in the glasses.

Sometimes the grown-ups stayed out there a long time, and Kate would fall asleep hearing them, but not hearing the words, just the lull of their voices. There was her mother's tone, like she was singing, though she wasn't. It was her way of speaking with airy notes that seemed to hook one word to the next. Her voice moved over and around some of the men's tones, or broke through and the men would stop to listen.

Jeff Driver's sound came in little bursts and stutters and sometimes if there were more grown-ups, like the Lordes from down the road, if they were also there, Jeff's sounds would be very easy to pick out because he was nervous around groups. He had a stopping sound he made, like he couldn't get around a ball in his mouth.

Her father's timbre was smoother, and she heard him less because he was a quiet man who took his time in saying things, and only said what was necessary. Though sometimes he could be very silly and make everyone laugh. It took you a little off guard and gave you a happy feeling.

The grown-ups laughed and chairs moved. The loose spring on the screen door jingled, and Kate listened, but the door didn't close all the way. The spring was broken. It would be Jeff Driver coming in. It would be him because if it were her mother or father they would pull the door to, and then there'd be a clunk, but there was none this time. Jeff was inside using the bathroom and her parents were quiet outside on the porch. This was before Jeff Driver and her father went down to Leah Flats for a game of poker.

Before this, before they went to bed, she and David had joined the grown-ups on the porch. They'd had cool drinks too, lemonade. Moths fluttered against the outside lamp, and the air was thick and they knew it would start raining again. More rain was coming, but it was nice to have this little break, and sit outside in the still air. There was no breeze at all.

Kate sat next to her father. He smelled of kerosene from washing his hands in it, trying to clean the stain off. Earlier in the day he'd stained the table in the back room—a picnic table he'd built with long benches attached. It looked funny in the back room, but soon would be put outside in the yard.

He wore jeans with a hole in one knee and Kate stuck her finger in the hole to tickle him. He let her do that for a while, pretending it didn't tickle, but she knew it did because the pitch in his voice rose just a little, and she ran her fingernail lightly over the soft skin just below his kneecap, and then he grabbed her hand like it was a little mouse, or a spider, and brought it to his mouth like he was going to eat it. She shrieked and pulled her hand away and there was some of his spit on her fingers because he'd put them in his mouth. She wiped her hand on his leg and said, "Yuck."

Jeff Driver laughed, *guff guff*, and Kate's mother smiled, and they all sat back and listened to the sounds of the night and the thundering brook down in the valley. David sat in the rocker and there was also that noise of the runners clacking on the wood floor and one of his heels scraping back and forth. David didn't laugh because he was always a little annoyed with Jeff for no reason—maybe this time because of Jeff's laugh. David didn't laugh, but Kate could see his eyes were bright and he was happy to be there.

It was just an evening on the porch. Soft light spread across the worn floorboards, dropped to the stone steps. The light waned on the walk, and surrendered to the blackness out there in the yard. But up on the porch they were in a cove of light. And the light draped over their arms and outstretched legs, and made elongated shadows that flowed from the bottoms of their chairs. Kate looked at the faces of her mother and father and brother and Jeff. There was an ease in her mother's face, but also a weariness around her eyes. People always said she had her mother's eyes. Kate gazed at her mother's face and it was as if she could see down through the years to when she'd become a woman, a wife, a mother. There would always be pleasure in warm evenings on a porch, these quiet gatherings of people, family. And there would always be a sadness in it. There's always a sadness in happy, content moments.

Before they adjourned to the porch—*Shall we adjourn to the porch?* her father said with a pretend haughtiness as if he was addressing important people, royal people—before they went out to the porch, they'd eaten supper. There was venison and macaroni, and the spirals of green fiddleheads that her mother had harvested from the woods. The smells of garlic and rosemary rose from the oven, and when they ate they tasted those things too.

Before supper there had been the day. Kate and David watched the brook, and then they'd crossed the field and four deer grazed there. The deer caught their scent, jumped and fled, though one stopped at the edge of the woods and looked back with shining eyes. Then it leapt, and they watched its high white rump bob until it disappeared between the trees.

David said, "Remember that story Dad was telling us about the woman who was a deer?" It was a bedtime story they hadn't heard in a long time because they read books now, but it was good to remember the story and made Kate want to follow the deer that had hesitated; maybe it was asking them to follow. Kate was ten years old, but she still liked to believe in things. She liked to believe that animals could talk to you with their minds, that beaver had elaborate mansions inside their stick huts, that there were fairies living in the poplar trees. She knew those things weren't real, yet there was something about being able to pretend, allowing herself to pretend, that felt like doors opening in her heart. Being ten was a very good age, she had decided. She was happy and she wished that when she died she would be ten in heaven, no matter what else happened to her in her life, or how pleased she might be at other ages, she must remember that ten was the best and that she should be ten in heaven, if there was such a place.

They left the field and crossed over the brook on the bridge the loggers had built, so it was stronger than most, and could hold huge trucks loaded with hardwoods. When they came up the hill to the cabin they saw their father hiking down. He was coming from his writing shack next to the cabin. He'd built the shack so he could have quiet while he was writing articles or books, and he went there in the mornings and closed himself in. Sometimes Kate stood on tiptoe and peered through the tiny window. He sat in his chair and typed on the typewriter. Then he'd lean back and smoke, and stare at the wall. There was a little sill where a two-by-four crossed and on the sill he kept things: the skull of a raccoon he'd found picked clean, a piece of black mica, a dried polypore as big as a dinner plate, a dog she had made out of clay, and an old silver belt buckle. Then he'd turn back and type some more. If she giggled, he'd unlatch the door and talk to her for a few minutes, but only a few because he had to get back to work.

Now he was coming down the hill and they ran to him. He had brown stain on his fingers. He said, "How's the brook looking?" And he wanted to go see it. It was exciting to go with their father, to show him the brook as if they'd discovered it. They told him they'd seen four deer in the field, and he nodded, proud of them for knowing that seeing deer was a special thing. Kate knew the things he loved and so she wanted to love those things too. Like spotting deer, or the bear claw marks on the apple tree, or moose track. Or the brook swelled and running out of control. A porcupine asleep and curled into the crotch of a tree like a huge bird's nest. The rain sweeping down the mountain and across the valley in a sheet until it rattled over the cabin roof. The smell of the woods just before rain, and after rain. The sun when it sank behind Cascom Mountain, and mostly that moment when the last ray wavered and held at the ridge, then went down, like it had been swallowed. Fireflies blinking above the field like stars going on and off.

The three of them watched the brook, and they showed him how the big rock was completely submerged, and you'd never know it was there except for that dip in the water just below it. He said, "We used to swim here, your mother and I, before you were born."

The deer were gone, and no more came.

They went on up the logging road, away from the brook, and the sound of the water diminished. Their voices sounded brighter in the quiet woods. They went past where any regular cars could travel, where it got steep and muddy and the grass grew like the hair on a Mohawk right down the middle. They climbed to the top where there was a view and they could see the cabin below with its shed roof and windows like eyes. Kate thought about her mother inside and that she was making supper for them, and also for Jeff Driver who would be coming from his job in the fire tower. Jeff usually came on Saturdays before he and her father went to Leah Flats to play poker with some other men.

In the clearing at the top of the ridge they stopped to look at the marker where they'd buried their beagle a few years earlier. The beagle had been shot by someone, no one knew who, and it was sad to remember what a good dog he was and also it was sad to remember that even in this sunny opening in the woods with the yellow grass, and mica glinting in the outcroppings of granite, there was someone out there who could shoot a dog.

They looked at the marker, then went on up the ridge to the old cellar hole where Zach Bean's great-grandfather had built the first farm on Mount Cascom, when the land was mostly fields and not so grown up with trees. Zach had sold these acres at eight dollars and thirty cents each, so now her father owned this land, all the way across the field and over the brook and up the hill to the cabin. Bushes grew at the rim of the cellar hole next to lopsided stone steps that led up to nothing. Saplings had taken hold down inside the foundation and grown taller than the hole was deep. Branches reached above the crumbling walls, and some of the rocks had tumbled down into piles. It was from this place that her father and mother had hauled a long piece of cut granite for the mantel above the fireplace in their cabin.

They sat and dangled their feet into the cellar hole. Kate was in the middle between her father and her brother. Her father sat close and his legs went down, longer than hers, and David's too and she felt small next to them. There was some dirt turned up in a pile and shovel markings down there where people had been looking for artifacts.

David had found some china fragments in the ground a few yards away, and one time he'd been very lucky and discovered the silver belt buckle. But most of the cellar holes around the mountain had already been excavated by people who stayed at the lodge across the valley, and there wasn't anything left to find.

Kate leaned forward. The base of the old chimney still stood and orange daylilies grew in a tuft. Once there was a kitchen and a stove where Zach Bean's great-grandmother set a kettle to boil. And there were rooms where children slept and whispered to each other, and then fell quiet, listening to the comfortable murmur of adult voices. A family had lived here and ate and slept, and much more than that. It was strange to sit here and imagine people walking around and moving through invisible rooms. What if they glanced up and saw Kate and David and her father looking in?

Kate leaned out. There was a rusty barrel down there for some reason. She stretched to see more, and then she was falling head first into the hole. Someone clutched her shirt and yanked her back. Her collar came up tight on her neck and it hurt, also it hurt where the hands grabbed her. David's fingers dug into her arm. Her father's hand went into her stomach. Her father gasped and said, "Oh," in a way that sounded like he was falling himself, just catching himself from falling. It hurt how they seized her and for a moment she felt angry. But her father had made the noise, and now she saw how she'd scared him. She knew he would not want her to fall or be injured. He'd made that noise and she felt his arms around her, squeezing her, pulling her back onto the bristly grass away from the edge. He let out his breath.

"Be careful, Katy," David said, annoyed, and in a way that was nothing like the sound, the "Oh," her father had made, or the "Oh" she'd said at the same time, as if they were one person falling when it had only been her.

Then her father said, "We should head back."

Before this day there were many days, like the day Jeff Driver found the beagle lying dead on the trail, and how he wrapped the dog in a blue blanket, carried it to them like a baby. Or when Peter Lorde drove his big truck through the little poplar trees to make a road, and how they popped as they broke and flattened under the tires. Or when her mother and father held each other and circled the living room to the beat of a scratchy blues record, and how he lifted her and stood her on the table and held her hand so they danced like that, with him below, reaching up to her. And those nights when headlights came down the road flashing through the trees. And a kiss on the forehead and the sweet dream of a deer that could turn into a woman. Of believing in whatever you chose.

Though there were some things you would never want to imagine. Things you didn't want to believe could happen. Things that made the world never the same again, changing the last moments of before and before and before because they were the last hours, the last minutes, the last sigh and breath.

The Woman in the Woods

DAVID SAW A WOMAN STANDING IN THE WOODS near the trunk of a fallen tree. She might not have ever noticed him if his dog hadn't gone up to her, sniffing and wagging his tail. Jolly wasn't a mean dog—just a mutt David had rescued from the pound one year. Thankful ever since, the dog greeted everyone he met. He stuck his nose under the woman's coat, his hind end swinging back and forth. David had to call Jolly off.

There was a shell of snow over the ground. It was dry and crusty, broken open in patches. The woman wore low boots, the kind that were wide around the ankles as if they were meant to catch something or her legs had grown too thin for them. They weren't right for these woods. She had on a pinkish-colored coat—soft looking—more like a housecoat. When she turned to see whose dog it was, the coat swung open. Underneath she wore a blue dress. It was cold out and David wondered why she didn't button up.

But it was none of his business. He got hold of Jolly and said he was sorry. "He's only saying hello," David said. "He won't hurt you." The woman just looked at the dog. David couldn't tell whether she was angry or frightened. "Sorry," he said again as he rubbed Jolly down the back a few times to let him know he was appreciated.

The woman's mouth opened a little. It was small, not much wider than the spread of her nostrils. Her upper lip dipped in the middle, exaggerating where it rose into two points. From a distance you could imagine that there was a pink moth stuck over her mouth. Some moths, he'd read in school, live for only one day. Her eyes, dark and far apart, fell on him for a moment, on the .22 he carried under his arm, then she looked away and tilted her head as if she were trying to see through the trees. That was one reason he liked Little Spur Trail: you could see a good distance between the trees. He always carried his .22 when he was in the woods, even when he wasn't hunting. Lots of men carried guns when they were in the woods; his father had. David couldn't think of what to say to her, so he moved off, wondering if she was watching him as he walked away.

There was a story his father used to tell when David was little. It was about a woman who was really a deer. She appeared mysteriously and a family took her in. One night while the woman slept, the children lifted her skirts and saw deer hooves instead of feet. David's sister Kate had always wanted to hear that story. Occasionally his mother helped their father tell it as she sat on the end of the bed where they were all snuggled together. David liked to feel the weight of his father's arm on his shoulder as he listened to their voices—the way one spoke, then the other. His father would get a strange gloss over his eyes as if he were staring at something far away. And when his mother added parts, his father watched her and nodded, as if the story were really true.

Jolly picked up a scent and took off on his own as David continued up the mountain. He heard the dog howl in the distance, but after a while, the only sounds were the trees creaking and his boots crunching the ground. A wind had come up, squeezing itself through the branches and into his sleeves. He had on long underwear and a good coat but still his arms were cold. They tingled with "angel fingers," as Kate would say. *I've got angel fingers running over the top of my head,* she'd say if she got a chill. Sometimes they'd come around her neck. Angels with icicle fingers. His mother said they touched her too—she was cold all the time. She was so skinny; there was no meat on her bones to keep her warm. Kate and David always tried to get her to eat more. Their father was dead—long since buried; maybe he was the coldest of them all.

David kept moving. He wondered about the woman; she probably wasn't from around here. Maybe she'd come a long way to be alone—to get away from other people. She wouldn't stay out long. It was less than a mile down to the main road from where he'd seen her. She probably drove some kind of car like a Buick or a Cadillac. It wouldn't take much time to heat up. In just a minute she'd feel warm air on her legs, filling the car.

She wasn't that old, but it was hard to know exactly. There were girls at school who could walk right into the liquor store over in Wentworth Junction and buy whatever they wanted without anyone asking anything. They just looked more mature than the boys their age.

Since his father died, most people treated him older. His mother called him the man of the house. It didn't sound right and made him feel a pit in his stomach. When he looked in the mirror, he didn't see a man—just a boy with skin that seemed too small for his face, pulled tight and red under his nostrils and around his chin—only a few fine hairs. He wished he could grow a beard to hide in. He'd kissed a girl once: Meryl

Beaulieu. When they pulled apart, he stumbled backward. After that, whenever Meryl came around, he opened his locker and stuck his head in as if he were searching for something.

From the top of Little Spur, he could see Cascom Mountain through the trees. Usually, from a distance, the summit looked like a giant snow-covered breast, the fire tower on top sticking up like a nipple. But from this view it looked flattened out and tipped sideways, like a boat full of water or a rotten squash with the stem sunk in.

He didn't stay on Little Spur long. The wind pushed at him with one steady blow so he could practically lean against it. He got down fast, back into the protection of the trees. It was there that he saw the deer. At first he thought it was just the sprawl of some roots pulled out of the ground from an overturned tree, then it moved. It was a doe. Its eyes were smooth and bright like stones under water. It was looking at him but maybe didn't recognize his shape yet because it didn't seem afraid. If it was deer season, and he had his .30-30, he might shoot, and then they'd have venison all winter. His father would shoot. He'd shoot it clean. But there was one time, his father had told him, that he'd only wounded a deer. He had followed it for miles into the night, using a flashlight, stopping to examine the ground and low leaves where red blood marked its trail. He'd tracked it all over the mountain and into the ravine, where he found it by the brook and ended its suffering. *It's best to kill them clean*, his father said. *But if you don't, you are responsible. Never leave an animal to suffer a slow death.*

Now, the doe lifted one of its sharp narrow hooves and took a step toward him. It raised its snout a little, giving the air a sniff. David wondered where Jolly was. He hadn't heard him in a while. Then the doe jumped and its powerful legs carried it across the slope. It zigzagged between the trees until it was gone. But it wasn't Jolly who scared the doe off; it was the woman, down below, coming up.

She walked with her arms folded across her middle, her coat held closed. The terrain was steep and icy; she moved slowly, watching the ground, placing her feet carefully. With her arms crossed, her balance was off. Sometimes she swayed too far to the side and there'd be a hesitation in her movement as if someone had her by the shoulders, pulling her back. Then she'd draw herself forward, breaking free to take another awkward step up the trail.

She wasn't dressed for this weather. No hat. It wasn't right. David wiggled his toes inside his boots to make sure he could still feel them—they were stiff and thick. He should head home, get warmed up, but now he had to wait for the woman. She was slow. With her arms wrapped so tightly around herself, she looked like a mummy.

The woman glanced up and saw him. She turned quickly, lost her balance, and fell. She rolled a few feet, then slid several yards down the hill until she was stopped by a clump of young birch trees. At first David wondered if he should just walk away, act like he hadn't seen her fall so she wouldn't be embarrassed, but then she didn't move, just lay there, and he knew it wouldn't be right to pretend that nothing had happened. He dropped his rifle and pack and ran, half slid, down the hill.

He knelt next to her. "Are you all right?" he asked. She turned her eyes to him but made no attempt to move or answer. Her arms were still crossed as if she didn't dare undo what warmth they made, or kept in.

"This isn't a very warm coat," he told her. She looked away. He didn't know what to do. The leg he was kneeling on was growing icy right through his pants and long johns. "You ought to get up," he said, "before you freeze to the ground." Again she made no response. He looked up the hill. His pack and .22 lay in a pile. And from the place she'd fallen and slid, there was a pink tinge on the snow, left by her coat.

"Get up," David said and pulled on her shoulders. Her mouth fluttered open, then closed. "Please," he said. "Are you hurt? Should I go get help?"

Her lips moved as if she were swallowing something dry. She closed her eyes and he saw fine veins that trailed across her eyelids, fading out in the shadowy recesses like fishing line in deep water. In his father's story, when the woman was asleep, and after the children saw the hooves, they lifted her eyelids and saw waterfalls instead of irises.

David smelled cold air coming off the woman's coat, and other odors—moss, heavy with water. Her nose, like a piece of ceramic, was small and sharp with dark, half-moon nostrils that moved slightly as she inhaled. She opened her eyes. Little shapes moved and flickered inside them. He looked away, down the length of her body, wondering how he could lift her into a sitting position. Her bare legs, laid out on the snow, looked hard and stiff like a doll's. And then he noticed that one of her boots was twisted sideways.

"Your boot's coming off," he said as he reached for it.

Suddenly she scrambled to sit up, holding her coat closed with one hand. Startled, David sat back on his heels and let her straighten it herself. She breathed heavily, then leaned to the side and got to her feet.

David also stood, and brushed the snow off his knees. He couldn't help but stare at her legs. She let her coat hang open and he could see the blue dress, made of some light material.

Her braid hung over her shoulder and she flung it back. Now David saw her neck and how thin and white it was. There were swirls of brown in her eyes that reminded him of knotholes in the pine ceiling above his bed. She was pretty in a way, but older than he was. Maybe she was as old as Miss Lemieux, his French teacher at school. Miss Lemieux was pretty in a way, too, if you didn't think of her as a teacher.

The woman's lips closed; she shivered. He could tell that she clenched her teeth together to stop her chin from trembling and that's how it sounded when she spoke—like her teeth were locked tight, making it difficult for words to come out.

"Go home," she said. "Leave me alone."

Now he felt his shoulders begin to shake and his knees as well. Where was Jolly? Usually by now he would have run the rabbit back toward David. Or he would have come back anyway just to check in.

The woman looked toward Cascom Mountain like she wished she could go there, or he was holding her back. David's whole body shivered out of control. He took a step back, then started up the hill to fetch his pack and .22. He stamped his feet to warm his toes and watched as she leaned against one of the birch trees. She turned away, arms hanging, coat still open. When he came alongside her, going down again, she acted like she didn't even know he was there. The cold bit the back of his throat, bringing up the faint taste of blood.

He'd gone about two miles across the valley. Soon he'd hit the Wilderness Trail and head home. Jolly howled off in the distance. It was growing dim in the woods, and David wished Jolly wasn't so far away, but the dog couldn't help himself—it was his instinct to hunt.

Icy air hummed as it sifted through the trees. The pines, towering above, moaned, their sap rigid and near frozen inside, then they became still as if bracing for a storm. He wanted to get home, but he shouldn't have left the woman. It was too cold. On the Wilderness Trail, he'd double back to Little Spur, see if she had made it out.

The sky was still light gray, but it was dark under the trees. He had a flashlight in his pack. He took it out and turned it on, scanning the ground for any sign. In the story his father used to tell, the family was starving; the father was deathly ill and unable to hunt, and the mother was growing weaker. They still shared what little they had with the woman. Then one night, the children watched from their loft as the woman lifted her skirts over her head and stood naked in front of the fire. Her legs were covered with brown fur that disappeared into her boots where they knew she had hooves instead of feet. And the skin on her back was cracked and leathery like salted hide. When the woman opened the door, naked, but upright with her fur legs and black boots, there was nothing to do but go after her.

Jolly returned and ran ahead, then back, as if trying to draw the slack taut between them. David moved faster, stepping carefully on the slippery terrain. Jolly sniffed the ground frantically as if unable to determine the start of a trail. When his head came up into the beam, his eyes were glowing beads, caught in the light. Then he was off.

At the top of the hill, where David had last seen the woman, he stopped and turned, then shined the light down through the trees. He thought he could see a pink hue on the snow near the stand of birches. He was sure the woman was somewhere near. Maybe even just over the next bluff.

He walked slowly, shining the light all around. She had no reason to stay on the trail, but he couldn't leave it. If he did, he'd surely get lost.

And then it started to snow. He turned the flashlight up; the tunnel of light caught the edges of pine boughs, then faded into the black sky. The snowflakes came down the beam, twirling and spinning. He watched them and tried to see up through to where the snowflakes began, but his gaze was inevitably drawn downward. He felt them land on his face.

"Hello?" he called out softly, hearing the strangeness of his voice in the woods. Then louder, "Are you here?" No answer. It was foolish. You could never find someone in the woods at night. And now it was snowing hard. He turned around and headed back. The sound of his boots grew muffled in the new snow. "Where are you?" he said as he went on. "I don't want you to die."

The wind picked up and ice crystals mixed with the snow and pelted his jacket. His fingers felt numb inside his mittens and he clapped his hands together. You could not survive for long out here.

In his father's story, the children nearly froze as they followed the deer woman's footprints. They tracked her up the dark mountain and down. They knew she was their only hope for finding food. At the brook, near the waterfall, they came upon her empty boots standing in the snow. Around them, deer tracks disappeared into the water. They smelled rich soil, grass, and the musky smell of game, wafting through the secret tunnel under the waterfall. What happened after that? Nothing. David and Kate had grown out of bedtime stories. The tale was never finished and now he wouldn't ever know; the bridge had washed out in a flash flood and his father was killed.

Finally the cabin came into view. Smoke streamed from the chimney in thick gray folds and fell in wisps over the roof. They didn't live in the cabin during the winter, except for weekends, or school breaks, like this. It wasn't insulated, and the roads could be bad, but his mother liked it here better than their apartment over in Wentworth Junction, so they came often.

"Where'd you go?" his mother asked him when he came in. Her blond hair hung in dark, wet strands and left damp spots on her shoulders. She wore slippers and a faded red bathrobe. When she straightened her arms he saw where the points of her elbows left imprints in the knit material.

"Just around," he said. He thought to tell her about the woman, but he didn't know how to start. He shouldn't have left her on the mountain. He should have found her and brought her down.

"Get warm," his mother told him, meaning that he should stand by the fire. He did, toeing his boots off first and dropping his jacket on the bench by the door.

"Kate's making dinner. I'm not terribly hungry," she said.

"Sure," he said. He let the fire almost burn the backs of his legs before he turned around. His feet ached as they came back to life.

Kate stood looking at him. "Where's Jolly?" she asked.

"Out," he said as he opened the woodstove to throw a log in. He left the door open to give the fire air. He knew Kate worried about things, like Jolly being out at night. They'd had a dog long ago that had been shot by someone, no one knew who, or for what reason. The fire watchman, Jeff Driver, had found the beagle off a trail and brought him down. David's father had almost cried; he'd loved that dog, said he was the best hunting dog he'd ever had.

"He'll find his way and be home soon," David said more gently.

His mother stood near the front window. In the dim light her cheeks were hollowed, and her profile was sharp—a light behind her emphasized her thin figure. The window had moisture on it and white frost at its base where the glass didn't sit tight in the frame. It looked as though she'd run her fingernail through it several times. For a second he wondered if she'd written a word, but he couldn't make anything out. She put her hands into the pockets of her robe and her shoulders came up as she took a deep breath.

"I'll bring some wood in," he said.

She didn't answer, just turned her head like she was trying to see through the lines she'd carved in the frost. He turned on the outside light and leaned against the wall, then slid his feet into his damp boots and laced them. He kept one eye on her, wondering if she might stop him, but she didn't, and he went out, shutting the door behind him, then crossed the yard toward the woodshed.

It was dark in the shed, but the outside light reached through the door enough for him to see. Water had leaked through the roof and dripped onto the woodpile, freezing the logs together. He knocked one free and used it to loosen the others, then piled them in his arms. He thought he saw something: a piece of cloth or the toe of a boot sticking out from behind one of the stacks. His heart raced as he stepped back, peering around, sure to see the woman. But it was nothing, a piece of bark.

When he got back to the front door, it wouldn't open. He kicked it with his foot, reaching from below his armload and turning the knob; it was locked.

"Mom," he called. "Door's locked." He tapped it with his foot a couple of times. When it still didn't open, he took a step back to look at the window. He could see the scratches in the frost, and then his mother staring out through them. "Mom," he said loudly. "Open the door!" He saw her robe, a hazy red through the glazed glass. He moved closer to the window, shifting the logs in his arms and kneeing them up. Then he noticed her eyes, focused on something, past him, over his shoulder near the shed. He looked quickly and felt a wash of wet air cross his face as he turned into the condensation of his breath.

For a second, he saw the shape of a woman, her thin legs going into those wide-topped boots, but then she wasn't there and it was just gray lumber, leaning against the shed. When he turned back to the cabin, the door was open.

David and Kate ate at the kitchen table without speaking except for *Pass the salt please.* Kate made macaroni and cheese and it tasted good. Their mother had gone into her room as she often did around dinner time. Kate glanced at the bedroom door every now and then as if she'd heard something and thought their mother was coming out. Neither one of them liked to leave their mother alone. Not since she nearly starved herself to death a while back and had to get medical help. Now she ate, but often had to be reminded, as if those mechanisms—the basic ones that said, "Eat"—had been shut down or were off kilter.

He wanted to tell about the woman. He chewed some food and thought about what words he could start with. *I saw a woman today,* he might begin. Or, *There's a woman out there, I think.* But the more he thought about what he could say, the more he felt the words crumble in his mouth and dissolve.

Then Jolly barked and scratched at the door, and Kate hurried to let him in. He came in wagging his tail and nosed up to them, especially David, as if to apologize for not staying with him. Jolly jumped up, his paws on David's thighs, head bobbing. David scratched behind the dog's ears and gave him pats on his sides that made deep hollow sounds as if Jolly were empty, just hide pulled over ribs.

His mother came out of her room and Jolly went to her too, but she walked past him and sat near the fire. Then Jolly shook himself and lay down on the hearth at her feet.

For a while David continued to eat, but not tasting anything. He heard the wind scraping the edges of the cabin. The glass in the windows was like black ice. He imagined opening the door and finding her.

"There was a woman in the woods today," he said. "Out there." His mother and sister turned toward him. He'd spoken loudly, he realized. His mother stared as if he'd frightened her. "She's out there somewhere," he said. "But she's probably dead by now."

"What are you talking about?" his mother said.

"In the woods, near Little Spur. She was just *there.* She didn't have on the right clothing and I tried to tell her, but she wouldn't listen." It felt like the fire was too close, burning him. "She told me to get away from her."

"Why didn't you say anything before?" Kate asked.

He looked away. "I couldn't." The flames in the woodstove darted up like hands. "I went back, but she was gone."

"Are you sure?" his mother said. Her voice was low.

"Yes," David said. "I saw her. I tried to find her, but she wasn't anywhere."

"We have to find her!" Kate said. Her lips trembled.

"It's too late now," he said.

"No, she could still be alive. We have to go after her!" Kate turned from him to his mother.

"Kate, I searched," he said. "It was dark. I don't know where she went. I had to come home."

Kate began to cry and sat down on the hearth next to Jolly, who raised his head and licked her arm. David looked at his mother, but her eyes were fixed on the window as if she could see through the reflection into the dark. He wondered, suddenly, if she was thinking about his father. The accident had happened on a night like this, and they'd all gathered around, stunned by the news, half-thinking that there was some way to stop the truck before it had reached the bridge—to change everything and make it not real. His mother had said, *If only I hadn't let him go to town*, and *If only I'd gone with him.*

"I could go out again," David said.

His mother spun around. "No!" she said. "You'll do no such thing. Not on a night like this."

Kate looked up, her eyes wide, and he was sure that she, too, was thinking about that night their father was killed.

His mother stood and began to straighten his drying clothes and the chairs. There was relief in hearing her tell them what to do. "You don't know anything for sure," she said. "If the woman was out there, she probably came down. Maybe we can report it." But then she turned and went into her bedroom.

David's arms and legs felt stretched and overused. He heard Kate rattling dishes in the sink as he undressed and climbed into bed. Maybe his mother was right. But the woman *was* there. In the morning, he thought, we will find her dead.

ooooooooo

Branches in the pines rustled and rubbed their long green needles together like hands, like brooms sweeping the floor. David awoke to find Kate standing over him. Her face was narrow, pulled long.

"David," she said in a harsh whisper. "Someone's out there. Jolly's going crazy."

David sat up quickly, then held still to listen. It was gray outside, not dark but not light yet either. Then he heard it. It wasn't the wind. Kate grabbed his arm and squeezed. They stayed still, listening. He'd heard fawns before that sounded just like human babies crying. But this wasn't a fawn.

"Get Mom," he said as he shook Kate off his arm and reached for his jeans.

Jolly scratched and growled at the front door as David slid bare feet into boots, pulled on his jacket.

"David? What is it?" he heard his mother say from behind him as he stood at the door, trying to see. It was dim and dull like under a bed sheet. There was new snow, blown in drifts against the side of the cabin and at the base of the door. He stepped into the air and felt it wrap around him. Jolly was already past him, using his nose like a plow through the snow. He yelped—serious barks—on the trail of it, and David followed him, crossing the yard toward the shed, and then back toward the corner of the cabin, where the woman lay like a rag doll, swept against it—her head and shoulders tipped over on herself, her legs straight out.

Jolly got to her first and sniffed wildly at her legs. David bent over her and, with his fingers, touched her forehead. It could have been ice.

ooooooooo

His mother worked fast. She dialed the phone and at the same time yelled directions at them. "Get your sleeping bags," she said. "Lay one on the floor in front of the stove." They'd dragged the woman, the three of them, by her arms and shoulders into the cabin, then managed to lift her into a chair, where she folded over herself again. Snow turned to water across the floor. His mother was on the phone, telling someone to come, and then she held the receiver away and said, "Take her coat off. Take her boots off."

Kate raised the woman's arm and began to work at the coat. David lifted one of her legs by the calf, felt the weight of it in his palm. The boot, full of snow, came off easily. Her feet were small. He put his fingers around them and squeezed gently. The toes—little white stones—were rigid and hard. Her eyes were closed and her head bobbed as Kate tugged the ends of her coat sleeves.

Kate began to cry as she struggled. His mother helped, lifting and pulling. Once the coat was off, his mother slid her hands under the woman's arms and hoisted her out of the chair. The woman flopped against his mother, her toes dragging through melted snow, and then his mother lowered her to the sleeping bag.

"Get close to her," she told them. "Lie on top of her. Get your skin against hers. We've got to warm her up."

For a moment David looked at his mother; her bathrobe beneath her jacket was wet and clung to one of her thin legs. Her eyes were wild, shining. She held up the other sleeping bag, and pulled at the zipper to open it up. "Lie down," she told them. "Go on."

They knelt slowly at first, each on either side of the woman, and stretched out and put their arms over her. His mother covered them with another sleeping bag, sealing them together in a cocoon. Kate's arm overlapped his arm across the woman's chest. He and Kate had lain like this with Jolly before—cuddling him as he slept.

"I'm not sure what to do," he heard his mother say as she tucked the sleeping bag around their feet. "I'll heat some water. Stay close to her," she said from the kitchen.

David pushed his body closer to the woman, and lay one leg over hers. He could feel her breast under his arm. She was breathing. There were little noises—whispery moans. He pressed his face into her neck and blew warm breath against her. Kate moved too, and adjusted her body against the woman's. He thought of their heat, leaving them and going into her. He thought of her blood starting to loosen and flow, moving around and through her heart. Under his palm, near her throat, he felt a pulse. His lips touched her neck and he moved them against her skin as if speaking, but not with sound or words.

His mother settled near their heads. "We've got to get her body temperature up," she said. "I wish they'd hurry."

David and Kate shifted as their mother eased her hands under the woman's head and propped it against her knees. She held a mug to the woman's lips. The woman's eyes were still closed, but she swallowed, then made a noise.

"Is she saying something, Mom?" Kate asked from the other side of the woman, under the sleeping bag.

David raised his head to see better. The woman's eyes opened, small crescents of dark water. "Ahh," she said. They waited for her to say more. "I heard you," she said to David.

The woman's eyelids fluttered as the rim of the mug touched her again. Had she heard him? Out there, in the night, when he'd called to her? Is that what she meant? Had he led her out after all? He tucked his head down under the edge of the sleeping bag and tightened his arm around her. *I heard you*, he mouthed silently, his lips against her shoulder. He concentrated on feeling all the places where his skin touched hers. Those places felt hot, but he knew they weren't. If things were strong enough, your senses could get mixed up. In some ways he wished that the ambulance people would never come.

They heard the siren grow closer. His mother let the woman's head down, stood, and went to the door. The ambulance pulled into the yard and the siren died. Voices and footfalls came across the floor. David pressed his fingers into the woman's shoulder as the sleeping bag was dragged off.

"Move out of the way," a man said. Kate scrambled up. David's arm jerked. "Move!" the man said, and another man came around and pulled at his arm, helping him to his feet. Then the men knelt over the woman to work on her. David still felt the places where his skin had touched hers.

"She's unconscious," one man said.

"She was awake for a moment," David's mother said from across the room. She was standing near the door. A tall policeman stood next to her. "She drank a few sips of warm water," his mother said.

"That's a good sign," one of the men said, but then David saw him look at the other man, and then toward the woman's legs. "It will be a miracle," he said quietly, "if she doesn't lose these feet."

David pictured the colorless toes and her foot in his hand. There were old men from the paper mill who had lost fingers to the saws, their hands deformed, pincer-like claws. And there was Rick Genzer who'd come home from Vietnam without any feet. David should have led the woman down the mountain and fed her hot soup. They might have talked, and then maybe she would have leaned over and kissed him on the mouth, opening up a whole new world of hope. The men raised the woman's arms and pulled at her jaw. David felt as if he were watching from a tall pine tree, the ground spinning up to meet him. He moved back a step and braced himself against the bench.

"Are you okay, son?" It was the policeman next to his mother. They both stared at him. Then his mother smiled. His stomach felt weak.

"Going out," he said as he made his way toward the door.

The sun was melting everything. Water dripped from the eaves. The ambulance and the police car reflected sharp spirals of light in their windshields. David pushed away from the door and crossed the yard to the shed. It was dark inside and it took his eyes a moment to adjust. He picked a log off the pile and held it in his hands. Water dripped everywhere, coming through the cracks in the roof. Some dripped on his head.

David threw the log. It crashed against the wall and fell to the dirt floor. He picked it up again and swung it against the pile like a baseball bat. Other logs rolled and tumbled down at his feet.

"David?" It was Kate behind him. "What are you doing? Stop it, David." He gave the log one last swing, letting it go so it crashed and came to rest on the pile.

"Please," Kate said. "They're about to take her away." Her voice was soft and she shifted from one foot to the other. "The police chief said they've been looking for her. She's been missing for a while. He said her husband has been worried sick, searching everywhere for her." Husband? David hadn't imagined that she would have a husband. Behind Kate, the men moved quickly—one climbed into the back of the ambulance, the other closed the rear door and went around to the driver's side. The ambulance started up, lights flashing.

David moved past Kate into the yard, where his mother stood. He couldn't remember the last time he'd seen her outside. Her cheeks were flushed, and her hair was loose and laced with gold strands. She nodded at him, then raised her chin slightly, her eyes glowing. It was how his father had looked when they'd told the story—when his mother had added her parts.

"Mom?" he said. She blinked and tucked her hands into her jacket pockets. Behind her the ambulance pulled out of the driveway, followed by the police car. The sirens came on, loud at first, then more distant as they moved away. They'd take her to Northlee Hospital—a place he knew well. It was there his mother had stayed, hooked to tubes that fed her through her arms. And it was there they'd taken his father after the accident, although there was no need; he was already dead.

"Ooh," Kate whispered. "I just got angel fingers on my head." She lifted her arm and wriggled her fingers at the sky as if reaching through some hidden passageway.

"Our part is done," his mother said. "We probably saved her life."

David felt tears start. "She'll be a cripple!" he said. "She should have died. She wanted to."

Kate moved closer to him. His mother shook her head and looked from one to the other, then she took her hands from her pockets and held them out.

"No," she said, and at first he didn't know what she wanted—her hands raised toward them—but she waited and smiled as he placed his hand in hers.

"No," she said again. "No one really does." Her fingers tightened around his. Across the road, the culvert roared with water from a swollen creek, and Jolly, on the trail of something, howled in the distance. "Let's go in," she said. "We've had a hard night. We need some breakfast."

As they turned and made their way around ice and puddles, a cold air came up behind, at first trailing them, then draping over David's shoulders like the weight of an arm, trying to pull him into other invisible worlds. Or perhaps it only meant to guide him, all of them, as an act of rescue.

Wishbones

OUR FATHER ALWAYS CALLED MY MOTHER BEAN. She was slender and crisp. Now her cheeks sank in darkened hollows. Her nose was a pointy beak. I found her on the front porch, looking off toward the mountain. She flinched when I came up on her; then her arms trembled and one leg quivered in a little burst as if she had a chill.

"What are you doing, Mom?" I asked.

Her pupils caught the sun and glowed like owl eyes down a flashlight beam, glassy and haunted. She closed her eyes. She didn't want to talk. The ring on her finger was loose, and she slid it back and forth over her knuckle. When I sat next to her on the bench, her knee jerked to the side and almost touched mine, but not quite. Her yellow, corn-silk hair had faded, grown dull and ashy. It was the first time I really saw how changed she was, and it scared me.

It had been nearly two months since the bridge washed out and our father's truck had gone over. David was twelve, and I was almost eleven. We'd been trying to let her alone, not asking for things. Sometimes I thought she was afraid of us, like we might bump into her and knock her over. Or mention something she didn't want to hear about.

It was summer, and we lived in a cabin in New Hampshire that my father and mother had built together. They'd made it out of stones and logs. My mother mixed cement in a wheelbarrow, shoveling sand they'd hauled in a borrowed dump truck. She chopped down trees and skinned the logs with a drawshave. My father laid the stones and rigged pulleys to lift beams. Over the fireplace they erected a granite slab, dragged from an ancient cellar hole in the field below their site. On that slab my father chiseled, *Len and Carey built this house 1960* AD.

This was before David and I were born. Before our father finished graduate school, or got a job writing the "Outdoors" column for *Esquire*. Back then, when they were building, they didn't know about the future or where they'd settle down. They just wanted a place they could go to every now and then for a weekend. A place they could call their own. They had an apartment in Wentworth Junction not far from Grammie Hagen, but they went up to the mountain whenever they could. Later, our father became an instructor at the college just over in Northlee, near where we lived during the school year, though the cabin was always more like home. When David and I were little they put in a real bathroom. My mother knocked the outhouse down with a sledgehammer. She was glad to be rid of it.

"I'm going to get a Coke. You want one?" I asked her. She shook her head. I left her on the porch and went inside. David sat on the floor, working on a model of a dinosaur skeleton, the bones spread out around him. He acted as if he didn't know I was there.

"David," I said. "What should we do about her?"

"Hand me that glue," he said. He pinched two pieces of gray plastic between his fingers. I moved the rubber cement across the rug with the toe of my sneaker until he could reach it. Parts were laid out so you could tell how it would look when it was glued together. On the box it said, "Brontosaurus. Probably a herbivore," and underneath there was a picture of it, long necked, munching leaves off the top of a tree. A pterodactyl with batlike wings and a long snout full of teeth flew in the clouds above.

Birds, David once told me, probably evolved from dinosaurs. You could see it in their skeletons, how similar they were, with their curved, horny bills and clawed feet. David said we were all descendents of earlier species, like Cro-Magnon man. Which was easy to see, especially in some cases, such as Jeff Driver, my father's friend, the fire watchman, who had a big forehead and bushy eyebrows.

It had been two weeks since Jeff Driver stopped by, and I began to wonder if he'd show up tonight because it was Sunday, his usual night of appearance. Before the accident, we could have been assured of a visit from him on his way up the mountain to the fire tower. Usually he'd come right in without knocking, just a big "Hellooo" and then, "Miss Kate, you get prettier and prettier." Sometimes he'd say the same thing to my mother if he saw her first.

I thought about calling Grammie Hagen, but I remembered the last time she called and how my mother had told her that we were all right. My mother made her voice sing, even though she pressed her thumb between her eyebrows, like she had a headache. She said we didn't need anything and then she hung up. "Cow," my mother said, but it sounded like "caw" and made me think of cowbirds or blue jays—the ones that steal nests.

"She can be charming as hell if she wants to be," my father once said to my mother, "but when it comes to you, she's on the jealous side."

"Jealous side?" my mother said. "That woman *hates* me. She thinks her only son married a backwoods hick."

"No," my father said. "No, she doesn't. Really, she likes you. She's just envious because you have me, and you're pretty and thin and she's a fatso."

At that my mother said, "Really? You think so? I'm not too fat?"

"Cut it out," he said. "You're a bean, Bean." But now he wasn't here to say things like that.

My father was just bones by now, though I didn't like to think about that. Grammie Hagen said that when a person died he didn't need his body anymore. The soul climbed out and rose to heaven. There was a place near the mailbox where the soles of my father's shoes were printed in the mud. They stayed there for days, until the rain filled them and they melted away. One day I found tracks near the brook that hadn't been there before. They were the size of my father's boots and had a similar tread. I knew it was probably just some hunter, but I liked to imagine it was my father visiting earth, flying over it and touching down every now and then.

"David?" I said, looking at his dinosaur. "Do you think Dad knows what's going on, can still hear us maybe?"

"Don't be stupid," he said.

David had an idea: let her alone and she'd get over it. I had an idea: make extra food and leave it around the house. Chicken soup, spaghetti and tomato sauce. Let the smells go everywhere. Eat warm brown bread in front of her and say, "I can't finish this. Want some?"

David and I knew how to cook some things for ourselves: canned spaghetti with hot dogs cut up and mixed in; baked beans with hot dogs on the side. In the pantry there were boxes of pasta, cans of Spam, tomato sauce, corn, soup, and sardines. Sardines made David sick, but our father loved them, especially on crackers.

David said, "Why don't you learn to make macaroni and cheese? Ask her to help you."

I asked. She handed me a cookbook and walked into her bedroom. When she pulled her sweater over her head, her shirt came up with it. Her waist was narrow, and her pants were loose and hanging low. Before, she was fuller, smoother. Her lips were always on the verge of a smile. In the mornings when she used to fix my hair, her fingers felt like feathers at the back of my neck. When the braid was done, she'd pull the tassel end to the front and say, "Now let me sweep your face." All my father had to do was make a funny face and she'd laugh. "Stop! I can't breathe," she'd gasp, and wipe tears from her cheeks. It was contagious, and David and I would fall back in our chairs all Jell-O arms and shaking. Then, just when you thought it was over or things should be serious again, she'd turn a sigh into a giggle and start everyone into a fit once more. When you could open your eyes, you'd see how my father was delighted, and she'd be all rosy and glistening. Now she had a different face, the hard shell beneath coming through.

David and I ate crackers and cheese for dinner. We sat in front of the television. I kept thinking one of us would go over and turn it on, but we didn't. We just kept crunching, almost a whole column of Saltines between us. David sliced the mold off a piece of cheddar, and glanced toward the door.

"Do you think he's coming?" I asked.

David made a tower, alternating cracker and cheese. He picked up the top three pieces like a sandwich and took a bite. "Beats me," he said with his mouth full.

"Maybe he'll know what to do about Mom," I said and started my own stack.

"Do what about Mom?" David said. "The guy is a retard!"

I didn't know what to say. My father once said that Jeff was a bit off, probably because he spent a lot of time alone on the mountain. *But when it comes to forest fires,* my father said, *I've never seen anyone snap to action faster.* It was true. Jeff carried a walkie-talkie that crackled with voices I couldn't understand, but he'd zero in, ear cocked, hearing everything. I'd seen him run out in the middle of conversation and take off in his truck. Once my father mentioned Jeff in his column for *Esquire.* He wrote, "From his fire tower on top of Mount Cascom, Jeff Driver is an unlikely God, watching over our valley."

Once Jeff gave me a compass. There was no glass on it, and the arrow was bent, but he thought I might like it anyway. I did. It still pointed north.

David chewed with an angry look. "Maybe he could take her for a ride," he said. Little bits of cracker puffed out of his mouth. "He could drive her down the mountain and off a bridge. That'd fix things."

David's words made me wince. It was an accident, nobody's fault, I wanted to say, but I didn't. Jeff Driver wasn't even the one at the wheel that night he and my father went down to Leah Flats for a game of poker. Jeff hadn't done anything except come out alive.

David's chin twitched, and he sucked in his upper lip, making his nostrils widen and his jaw stiff. It looked like he was trying to make his face stay still.

"I'm going to see how she is," I said, and got up.

She was in bed, staring at the ceiling.

"Mom?" I said. "Do you want anything to eat?"

She turned toward my voice, but her eyes were dull—little ponds covered with film. I moved closer. When she swallowed a thin, V-shaped bone in her neck sank, disappeared below the surface, then bobbed up again. It put me in mind of a wishbone.

I owned a paper bag full of wishbones that my father had saved from all the birds he'd ever shot and eaten. He'd started collecting them when he was a kid. *Turkeys, ducks, grouse, you name it,* he'd said. They were brittle and brown—a snarl of Vs, hooked and crisscrossed, all different sizes. I'd been adding to them. First they dried in the sun. There was one from the partridge we'd gotten last fall still on the windowsill.

My father had taken me along when he went hunting. I followed him down the trail through the woods. When we came into the field, he said, *Now we walk quietly.* In my pocket I wedged the shotgun shells he'd given me to carry between my fingers so they wouldn't rattle together. I moved when he moved and stopped if he did. When the partridge flushed, beat its wings in a thunder, I nearly jumped out of my skin. My father raised the gun and fired.

I carried the bird home, dangling it upside down by the tail. It didn't weigh very much—maybe as much as a bunny. My father hunted deer and rabbit too. When we ate them, I didn't like to think about what they looked like before. I'd seen my mother skin rabbits, yanking their fur off like sticky gloves. And I had a rabbit's foot my father had given to me for luck. He salted the end to dry up the blood and keep it from rotting.

You didn't pluck partridge. The skin was soft so you could reach right in and pull the breast out. My mother cut the tail off first and spread it open so the black dots and tan shapes turned into zigzagged stripes. Later she tacked it to the beam in the back room next to all the others. One after another, a row of seventeen feathery fans.

"Partridge aren't the smartest birds in the world," my father told me. "They get panicky and fly up. But in the spring, when there are chicks, they know all sorts of tricks to distract predators away from their young. They'll pretend to have a broken wing and hobble around on the ground, try to lure you away from the nest. They'll even fly in your face." I was glad we didn't hunt when there were babies waiting for their mother, necks stretched and mouths wide open to the sky.

David was in the bathroom running water when I went back to my own room. I picked the partridge wishbone off the sill. I pretended that my right hand was me and my left hand was the other guy. I snapped it and I won.

"Please make my mother hungry," I said, and dropped the pieces in the bag with all the whole ones. I thought about breaking apart some more, but I didn't want to use them all up, or lose. Then I wandered into the pantry and began turning boxes of pasta around so the cellophane windows showed how much was left. That was when I heard Jeff Driver's truck pull into the yard.

David and I waited for the door to open. We looked at each other when he knocked. David turned the knob and let the door swing back as he walked away. Jeff came right in.

"How are you, Kate?" he asked me. He held his cap in his hands and looked down the hall that led to the bedroom where our mother was. "Is she asleep?" he asked.

I shrugged.

"Maybe I'll just stay for a while, until she wakes up," he said. He wore a brown uniform and smelled like the rain and woods.

"You can just go see her," David said.

"Well," Jeff said, "A man really shouldn't go into a lady's bedroom without her permission. I'll just wait." Then he sat at the table, laid his hands on it and laced his fingers together in a little fence in front of himself. Dark hairs puffed out in a fringe at his cuffs.

Grammie Hagen said that evolution was tommyrot, and we were never apes. She said that the fossils they dug up might be God's way of testing our faith. Or maybe, she said, the scientists planted them in a plot to tarnish the Word. Once Grammie Hagen gave me a charm bracelet with a tiny gold locket attached to it. Inside was the Lord's Prayer in print so small I had to get a magnifying glass to read it. I memorized it so when I was scared, I could recite the whole thing to keep away evil spirits. But since my father died, whenever I started, *Our father who art in heaven,* I didn't think of God, but rather, my father, who was, according to Grammie Hagen, within the kingdom.

"I don't know what you're waiting for," David said to Jeff, and plunked himself on the floor next to his dinosaur skeleton. He tapped the backbone with each of his fingertips like he was playing a slanted piano. "She's not going to get up," he said.

"That's okay," Jeff said. "I'm patient."

David closed his fist around the dinosaur's head and twisted it off. He unclenched his fingers one by one like he didn't really know what was in his palm. Then he flung the piece on the rug and looked at me. At first I thought he was scared, like he couldn't believe what he'd just done—breaking apart what he'd worked so hard to put together. Then I realized he'd caught sight of something else.

Our mother had come out of her room. She wore nothing but underwear. There was a shirt in her hands. Ribs, sharp and clear, cut around her sides. Her collarbone sliced across to her shoulders like a hanger, connecting the bones of her skinny arms. Her breasts hung empty. She hadn't seen us. Jeff made a hiccup noise, and she jumped, clutched the shirt to her chest. Then she ran away from us, all knees and hips and elbow Vs. She made it to the other end of the hall and slammed the door.

Jeff got to his feet. Neither David nor I moved. We sat still, as though nothing had happened, as though my mother hadn't just fled down the corridor mostly naked. Hot spiders crept up my back and turned cold on my neck.

"I'm sorry," Jeff said, but I wasn't sure who he was talking to. "Geez," he said. "Jesus, Carey. What in the name of . . ." He stared at the bathroom door. There was no light under it. She was in there, in the dark. Jeff tipped his head, listening. He scratched the underside of his chin. Then he said, "Your mother's going through hard times. You need to take care of her." He had one hand on the edge of the table, leaning on it, his fingers spread out, the joints pressed white.

"We do," I said. The words came out so tight my scalp tingled. I tried to think of what else to say and wished David would help, but he turned away.

"Okay," Jeff said, and put on his hat. "Well, okay, okay." He poked his glasses straight. "Okay," he said again, like it was a piece of something stuck in his throat. "Do you need anything next time?" he asked. "Supplies?"

We didn't answer. I was thinking that supplies meant toilet paper and batteries, and I was thinking that next time was a long ways away. There was moisture on Jeff's forehead, and when he wiped it he knocked the brim of his cap, set it crooked. He didn't put it right. Then he left, backed out the door and went across the yard. We watched until his truck started, and the headlights came on, sending out yellow shafts full of bugs and moths, suspended in the light.

David looked sick. "Everything's all screwed up," he said. At first I thought he meant the dinosaur because he was staring at the head, but then his mouth went sideways, and he said, "What the hell is the matter with everyone?" and I knew he was talking about our mother and Jeff Driver. His eyes were full of water. Under my breastbone I felt a hard thing lodge in my heart and block the blood that needed to pump through. I knocked on my chest with my knuckles.

"Breathe," he said.

I took some deep breaths until the plug inside slipped through.

We could still hear the rumble of Jeff Driver's truck as he headed up the mountain, back to his station where he knew what to watch for and what to do. A few minutes later our mother came out of the bathroom with the shirt on and walked back to her room. David and I just sat for awhile; then we went into the kitchen to look for food.

I warmed a can of soup and filled a bowl for her. David was in the pantry, staring into the cupboards. "Thinking of something," he said as I went down the hall.

I put the bowl on the night stand and tucked a pillow behind her head so she was propped up, then sat next to her on the bed and held the bowl close to her chin. I spooned up some soup, blew on it first since it was hot, and held it toward her.

"Tomato," I said. Her eyes were fixed on the wall across the room.

I passed the spoon through her line of vision, but she didn't follow it. "Jeff Driver's gone," I told her. "I don't think he's coming back." She didn't seem to hear me at all. I set the bowl down and stood up.

"We *need* things," I said. I wanted to grab her and shake her, drag her out of bed, but I didn't dare pull her skeleton arms. I leaned in. "You. Get. Up," I said, spitting breath on her cheek. "You eat!" I made a horrible monkey-face right near hers, imitating her. She didn't flinch. I gritted my teeth at her. "I hate you!" I said. Then I saw into her eyes. They were smashed mirrors, dead, not looking out. Not back. "I hate you," I said again, but the words wobbled, and came out soft.

Now we walk quietly, I heard my father whisper. I felt dizzy and lay down on the floor next to the bed. After a while my arms grew tingly. Dishes rattled in the kitchen. I wondered if David was cooking something. New potatoes. Fresh peas. Cucumbers in vinegar. Warm biscuits. Strawberries and cream. Green beans, butter dripped over them. I could taste things. I thought I smelled fish.

My mother sighed, then there was nothing. No breath. I scrambled to my feet. My arms were weak, numb feeling.

"Mom?" I leaned close to her, but I didn't hear anything. "Mom!" I shouted, and she sucked air back in. Her eyelids fluttered, then closed. She made a clicking sound with her mouth and rolled away from me, onto her side. I straightened the blanket and smoothed it against her. I felt bones underneath and pressed down a little. They seemed to give, like hollow quills, not hard as I'd imagined them to be.

In the kitchen David was eating sardines out of the can. When he looked up, a bit fell off his fork onto the table.

Behind him was the wall and all the stones my father had placed so carefully, fitting each one with the next. He'd lifted, and turned, and thought about every stone. He'd put them together to make a wall, which became a house. And my parents had moved in, and David and I were born, and many things had happened.

The stones started to move, though I knew they were cemented together and strong, and would probably stand long after we were gone, just as that old cellar hole still lay in the field, like bones, like proof of a life. I focused my eyes and made the walls still.

"I'm calling somebody," I told David. He stopped chewing. I picked up the phone and dialed zero. David lowered his fork. I thought he was going to come across the room and stop me when I said to the operator, "Get me the police," but he didn't. "Yes," I said. "I think my mother is dying. Yes," I told the woman on the line. "Just me and my brother. Cascom Mountain Road. I'm Kate. Kate Hagen."

Now David stood right next to me and put his ear close to my head. I angled the receiver so he could hear too.

"Listen, Kate," the woman said. "We'll get an ambulance on the way. Tell me why you think your mother is dying."

David shifted from one foot to the other. There were lots of things to say, but I didn't say anything.

"She won't eat," David said, lifting his chin toward the mouthpiece.

"It's been a long time," I added.

"Is she in the house? Did she collapse?" the voice said through the line.

I waited for David and he said, "No."

"She's in bed," I said.

"Okay," the woman said. "The EMTs are on the way. Don't hang up until they get there. When they get there, you tell me. They should be there soon."

"Okay," we both said.

I held the phone between our ears and we stood there, sometimes saying yes or no to questions she asked. She had us tell her about what we liked to do for fun and where we went to school. Every now and then she sent one of us to check on our mother. She asked where our father was, only she called him our *daddy.* It was not what we ever called him. David went on talking as if that was all right, but it made me feel like we were not who we were anymore. Sour spit came up in my throat.

I had called for help, but something else had been creeping through me—an evil that wanted my mother to be found out. Had wanted to punish her. She was going to get in trouble. What would they do to her? I felt sick and shaky.

Headlights flickered through the trees and swung into our driveway. I ran out the door, fast across the yard. I crashed into the man coming toward me and pushed away.

"She's better now," I told him. "You can go home."

"Everything's going to be all right," he said.

I started bawling. I said it was all a mistake. I tried to block his way. Then another man grabbed me around the waist and pulled me into his chest and carried me inside.

"It's all right," I heard him say. "Your mother needs some help. You were right to call. Shush, shush," he said and ran his hands over my head. Finally, when I looked, I found my mother. Her eyes darted over me, and I could tell she didn't know what was going on or who anybody was.

"She's severely dehydrated," one man said to the other, and I pictured the flat, dried bottoms of empty puddles—

smooth mud, cracking. "She's emaciated," he said, and I knew he meant bones—that she was just bones.

"You did the right thing to call us, Kate," the man said. "You're a smart girl."

I nodded.

Now we were all leaving. David answered questions about our relatives. He told the men that our father was dead—that he died in June during the floods.

We moved through the dark, down the bumpy road toward town. My mother was on a cot in the back of the ambulance with one of the men. Voices came over the radio, and the driver spoke, telling them we were headed south on Mountain Road. He said that our name was Hagen, and they should call Lucy Hagen, who lived in Wentworth Junction and was our grandmother.

I pictured Grammie Hagen in her house as she rushed around, pulling on her coat, one sleeve, then scooping up her pocketbook, then the other sleeve. When she got to the hospital, people would turn to see what was coming. She'd barrel in, boss everybody around with her I-told-you-so face. Grammie Hagen said that David and I were all that was left of her son. She said she could see him inside us.

I felt something in my stomach, wings flapping. I thought it was how you got when you were very hungry—ravenous—so sick and empty that you couldn't really imagine eating anything, yet you knew that you had to in order to make it go away.

"I'm hungry," I said.

"That's good," the man said. "When we get there we'll find you something. What would you like to eat?"

"I don't know," I said.

"How about a turkey dinner?" he said. "They have really good mashed potatoes with gravy and butter. What do you think?"

"We like mashed potatoes," David said.

"That's good," the man said. "That's really good."

I twisted around to see into the back of the ambulance. It was light in there. The other man sat next to my mother and held her wrist with his fingers. I could see where her part ran down the middle, separating her hair and fanning it over the pillow. I wondered if she knew we were being taken away from home.

David tugged my sleeve. "Sit still," he said. He took hold of my hand, and we held hands on the seat between us. I liked him so well then, and I felt better.

I watched the black sky overhead until I noticed a reflection, curved up the windshield. There was a rectangle of light and the blurry shape of the man as he hovered over the cot in the back. I strained, but I couldn't see my mother. She was too low. I found David in the reflection, chin raised, looking skyward, too. I wondered if anyone was up there keeping an eye on us, or maybe nobody was. David's mouth opened, but he didn't say anything.

I shut my eyes. I wished we could go back to the night our father went out, only this time there would be no rain, no flood.

"It won't be long," the driver said. "They'll take care of her." His voice was a whisper, like he was talking to himself or he wasn't completely sure.

The road turned to washboard, and the ambulance shuddered, rumbling over it. He tugged the wheel this way and that.

I noticed a gold band on his finger, and for some reason it made me say, "I'm never going to get married."

He coughed and checked his rearview mirror, straightened it, cleared his throat.

"Aw, now," he said. "Don't say that. A pretty girl like you?"

I felt embarrassed, as if I'd asked for a compliment. Then anger worked itself into me.

"I don't want to be pretty." I made the word come out like it smelled bad. I didn't know what word I wanted; I just knew pretty was not what I needed to be.

"That's all right," he said softly. He patted my knee. "I'll bet you could eat a horse."

"Bridge's coming up," David said.

"We'll get you some turkey, gravy, mashed—"

"There," David said.

In the headlights it looked even brighter than I remembered. Fresh lumber—pale planks and rails, not yet weathered. David's fingers tightened between mine. We went right over it—a whole new sound, a hush under the tires. Then thunder again when we hit gravel on the other side.

The Last Thing I Remember

I.

ONE NIGHT I HID AT THE EDGE OF THE WOODS and watched my mother emerge from Alexander's tent. I saw her push open the screen and step out in her fluttering white dress as if bursting from a cocoon. Her hair, even longer than mine, flew out behind her as she ran across the field. And her clothes, bright and glowing in the dark, seemed to lift her above the ground until she disappeared into the trees. Not long before, I'd seen the shadows of their bodies inside the tent, elongated, stretched on the sloping wall. Then I saw how those shapes slid across the canvas, spilled into each other and became one.

Alexander didn't appear. Not even to tie the flaps or zip the screen. Soon the light inside the tent dimmed and went out. For a moment I couldn't see the tent; it had been swallowed by the darkness. I lowered myself into the grass. Anger wove through my ribs and yanked tight. I was twelve years old. Since my father's death, my mother had become a frail being, and I'd done a lot of work to keep her alive, trying to get her to eat, holding her afloat with the will of my love.

Behind the tent, rising up against the moon, stood the frame of Alexander's half-built house. A cast of bluish light fell through the roof beams and made crisscross shadows down the stones of the chimney and over the platform. Coals still glowed in the campfire nearby. I stared at the embers until they blurred. I squinted to make flickering needles of light extend and shimmy. In this illusion, I made jagged yellow fingers reach for the lattice of two-by-fours and curl around the studs. But this was only a fantasy, a creation of my imagination and the haze through teary eyes. When I blinked, the fire shrank back to its place—all edges defined again.

But later that night I woke in my bed to find my mother's face above me. She told me to get up, get dressed, hurry. Then, as if we flew over the treetops, we were there in an instant, standing in the field where I'd been hiding only a short time before. Alexander's house *was* burning. Sparks snapped and slow liquid tendrils wriggled out from the hot orange center and looped back like a close-up view of the sun. My eyes ached trying to absorb the brightness. The tent shuddered, pummeled in the strong draft. I stared in awe and dread. A dull pain began in one of my temples—already a discomfort forming in my unconscious.

The next day there was nothing left of Alexander's house but a black charred mess, fallen into the cellar hole.

The fire was ruled an accident. "Gas can exploded," the Fire Warden told Alexander. "Probably left too close to your campfire or spilled." Alexander gazed at the smoking remains and shook his head. Perhaps he couldn't imagine he'd done something so unthinking. Maybe he just couldn't believe his bad luck. Then the Fire Warden drove off and Alexander was alone. He stood there, his long ponytail bunched through the rubber band. Black marks on his arms and face. I watched from the edge of the field. He remained in that position a long time. Days, I think.

Eventually Alexander packed his duffel bags, broke down his tent and left the town of Leah. He drove away, his Land Rover kicking up dirt on the mountain road until it became a tiny cloud in the distance. He headed west, leaving New Hampshire behind. I didn't think I'd ever see him again.

In my room I drew a pillow over my face and scrunched my eyes tight. I put my hand under my shirt and felt the ridges of my bones. I slid my fingers over my chest, pressing and prodding. I don't know what I hoped to feel. My forehead burned. My heart beat underneath my palm like an animal twitching inside me. An evil raggy-haired beast.

When my fever broke, my mother sat at my bedside. She placed a moist cloth on my head. I rolled away and faced the wall. I couldn't look into her eyes. I was afraid she'd see the creature looking out. Or worse, that it might turn on her.

There were very few people living on Cascom Mountain Road when Alexander first bought the land and began to build. We could hear his vehicle on the logging roads, chugging slowly over the rugged terrain as he hauled in supplies. If the wind was right, the sound of saws whined out of the valley. My mother listened and watched the hills as if at any moment something might leap out of the forest. I kept an eye on her.

It had been over a year since my father died. My mother was still thin, but getting stronger. She was eating; I watched to make sure. The garden had become her obsession. She spent her days tending it. She grew everything from corn to kohlrabi.

At dusk a thin stream of smoke would curl above the trees and we knew it was his campfire. My mother and I would be on the front porch by then, watching evening come on. In the shadows my mother's skin was so pale that she seemed coated with powder, like that fine dust on the wings of moths. She wore a multicolored bracelet my brother David had made for her out of gimp while he was at boys' camp for the summer. The band twisted around her wrist like a Möbius strip. Sometimes I'd take her hand in my lap and trace the flat side of the weave with my finger, starting at the one point and ending up in what seemed like the impossible same place.

Though I'm sure Alexander would have come by eventually, it was my voice that first lured him from the woods. Back then, I often amused myself by singing. I sang while doing the dishes, or lying in bed before I fell asleep. I sang to Mount Cascom as the sun sank behind its peak. On this particular day I climbed to the roof of the cabin and leaned against the chimney. I pressed my hands over my ears. It made the sound larger, closer—an echo chamber in my head. I shut my eyes, and it was as if I was in there—inside my skull—though I imagined it as a theater with a domed ceiling, balconies with carved cherubim. *I can see you now,* my father used to say when he heard me sing, *up there on stage, under the spotlight.* He'd pass his hand through the air, squinting as if seeing into the future.

When I opened my eyes, there was a man down there at the edge of our woods. He carried a white cloth in his hand. His chest was bare and tan, and his hair was long and the hazy yellow color of morning sun. He wiped his forehead with the back of his arm, then waved at me and came on toward our house.

"Thought it was an angel," Alexander told my mother. My voice had carried all that distance. "Just Kate," she said, and he took a step back to see over the eaves where I peeked from above. The cloth he held was a T-shirt and now he pulled it over his head, covering the smooth muscles of his chest, the pyramid shape from his broad shoulders to narrowed hips. He shook my mother's hand and she invited him inside. I scrambled down the ladder after them.

Alexander admired the view from our front window and my mother explained to him how she and my father had built the place by themselves without any power tools. They'd chopped down trees and sawed them into logs and skinned the bark off. They'd scavenged ancient stone walls for rocks and rigged a block and tackle to hoist beams. She showed him a photograph album of the construction. There was one picture of her wearing nothing but a bra and shorts. She was smiling over her shoulder, bent slightly and pushing a wheelbarrow. I felt embarrassed. Alexander's eyes scanned the page. "Here's Lendel," she said pointing to a picture of my father. He stood atop the chimney, his feet on either side of the hole, waving down at the camera.

Alexander walked around the living room inspecting the stonework. "This is brilliant," he told my mother. She touched her lower lip with the tip of her finger. Then she invited him to stay for dinner.

That night, after I watched Alexander's flashlight beam swing down the hill and disappear, I climbed the ladder to the roof. My father had often taken us atop the roof to watch for meteors. It was a shed roof so you could lie out on the still-warm shingles. I felt warm inside too, and light, like I was letting a rope slide through my hands, letting go of something heavy. I thought about the evening and all the things Alexander had said, and the way he'd looked at me and remarked again that he was sure it was an angel calling him with her song.

I let myself float up into the rivers of darkness that wove between the stars, going on forever. I wondered if there was anyone out there who knew about us down on earth. I wouldn't have minded believing in heaven, but I didn't know if I did. There was a boy at school who always said, "God is only in our minds," or, "We made God in the image of ourselves." If this were true, then why didn't we know everything, like the purpose of our existence, for example? I thought about my father. How could any mind, a lifetime of experience, just vanish? I imagined that all the answers to my questions were hidden deep in my brain, perhaps in that part we supposedly don't even use. Maybe there was a picture of God there too, like a painting on a wall in a room, simply waiting for my arrival.

The screen door below creaked open, then closed. It was my mother, headed for the garden. She'd taken to planting by the phases of the moon. I'd seen her calendars and charts. It was a science. To think something so far away from the earth could cause a tiny buried seed to set and shoot up faster, stronger!

There was the moon, hanging in the heavens. There was my mother down in her garden. I could see her shoulders rising and falling. I looked back at the moon, at its haunted face. *It will never be the same*, my father had lamented, as he gazed at the moon not long after Neil Armstrong walked on it, leaping in slow motion. I was little, but that stayed with me.

I got in the habit of visiting Alexander's site. I tried not to be a nuisance. I liked being with him, and he seemed to welcome my company. He slept in a green army tent made of musty smelling canvas. Inside there was a cot and a little table where he worked on his house plans under a kerosene lantern. Sometimes he drew diagrams on a large sketch pad. And every once in a while he put out tin plates and shared a jar of pickled herring and crackers with me.

He'd strung clothesline between trees near his campfire and his clothes steamed as they dried on the line. The first time I saw some blue jeans smoking, I was sure they'd caught fire and I beat at the legs, pulling them down. Alexander thought that was hilarious. He hung other things on the line—ladles, pots and pans. He clipped his blueprint up with two clothespins, held the bottom so the wind wouldn't catch it, and pointed to ells and entryways, explaining things to me.

Part of his substructure was an ancient cellar hole that opened up like a crater at one end of his plot. He used stakes and string to mark off rooms in the land next to it. He took me on a tour.

"This is the kitchen," he said as we walked through an opening into a square of land. "And over here is a closet and the stairs to the bedroom. And down there is the basement." He swung his arm toward the rock-walled well—the old stone foundation—as if presenting a panorama. He pretended to open a door for me and we walked through to a cordoned-off square of dirt, which I already knew would be the living room. With the string at our shins, I made believe there was a picture window and screwed my fists to my eyes like a pair of binoculars.

"Nice view," I said. The summit of Cascom Mountain peeked over the trees. When the house was done, he was going to clear some land to make his view even better.

Before it got dark, Alexander would send me home. I'd trudge up the logging road and cross the valley to our cabin. One evening my mother was in the garden. I watched her slide her fingers up a zinnia stem and hold its magenta head between her fingers. She scrutinized it, popped it off and dropped it on the ground. Then she moved to the center of the garden and stood there. She looked like a stalk of corn, her silky yellow hair draped over her shoulders.

"Where've you been?" she asked without looking at me. "Don't bother that man."

"I won't," I said and went inside.

My mother was thirty-eight and a widow. I'd always thought she was beautiful, but that night I saw how grief had drained her and made her worn and terribly old in my young eyes. Years later people would say she looked youthful for her age; they'd mistake us for sisters.

Alexander was twenty-eight years old—sixteen years older than I was and ten years younger than my mother. I could calculate those things well, but I hated arithmetic. Math is important, Alexander would tell me, when you are building a house. You need to measure things precisely, do your geometry correctly or your structure won't be level. It may seem all right at first, but a plank cut short, or a joint angled off, will make everything else fall out of alignment.

To make myself useful, I carried the coffee can full of nails to him, or handed him the level while he was up the ladder. "Thank you, madame," he'd say, reaching down to me. His pants hung low on his hips, often weighted on one side with a hammer attached to his belt. His skin grew darker and his hair lighter. I watched him—the way he sometimes shook his head back, an elastic between his teeth, smoothing his hair into a ponytail.

"You have nice hair," I said to him stupidly.

He said, "Well, so do you." And once after I finally stopped giggling and sat down flushed and smiling at him (he'd hung upside down from a beam scratching like a monkey and making monkey noises), he said suddenly, "You have the prettiest green eyes."

Alexander sawed boards, hauled rocks, and mixed cement in a wheelbarrow. Occasionally he hiked up to ask my mother questions about this and that. She taught him to add lampblack to the cement to darken it so the color of the stones would stand out. She loaned him chainsaw oil and an extra tarp. When the chimney was done, the shell went up, and he lugged a table and chairs onto the platform.

One day he and I sat there and had lunch. It was like sitting inside a rib cage, seeing out between the boards. Then the sky filled with dark clouds and the air grew heavy.

"It's going to storm," he said, and thunder boomed in the distance. Just as suddenly the rain came. We ran, hooting and laughing, into the tent. Water pounded on the canvas. We sat on his cot and then he lay down, and then I did, only so my feet were at his head and his were at mine.

"Your feet are filthy," he said, and grabbed my ankle, pinched my toes.

"Hey, cut it out," I said, and pulled away. "Besides, yours stink." I slapped his boot.

"No, they don't," he said, and let his heel drop to the floor with a thud. I listened to the rain. I liked the sound. It made me feel safe. I thought of my father because he loved a good downpour and it brought back a strange memory. This is the way I remembered it and told it to Alexander:

One night when I was very small there was a terrible storm. Water beat against the shingles so hard that the roof above my bed started to sag. Then, just before it crashed down upon me, my father charged in and caught it. He lifted the entire roof with both his arms above his head, water gushing around the edges, and forced it back into place.

Alexander listened thoughtfully and didn't question, even though this couldn't have happened. For the longest time I believed it had.

"He sounds like a good man," Alexander said. "I wish I could have known him."

The rain pattered on the tent. I reached to touch the canvas above my head, but before my palm came to it, Alexander sat up and took hold of my wrist.

"Don't," he said. "It'll leak."

"Okay," I said, but he held on as if he didn't trust me. "I won't," I said and tried to twist my wrist from his fingers. He sat there at the edge of the cot, staring down at me with a serious expression. I was suddenly aware of myself, my body inside my clothes.

Alexander didn't move. I had time to wonder what he was going to do. His eyes stayed on mine. He still gripped my wrist above my head. I felt something, like water rippling over me. It was his other hand, his fingertips touching my shirt, then my stomach under my shirt. I couldn't breathe or move. The rain was pounding and the air was weighted with the smell of dirt and wet canvas and cut lumber. I felt tiny under his hand, my breast in the center of his palm.

Alexander's lips parted and I could see a little gap between his teeth. His head tipped down slightly. I'd never kissed anyone, but I'd practiced on the back of my hand. He pushed my shirt up farther and lowered his head. His hair fell across my chest. I looked down on the top of his head, not sure what I should do. I felt his breath on my skin, his mouth on my skin. His fingers slid across my ribs and over the waist of my pants and just under the waist of my pants; it tickled. I squirmed. He raised his head and looked at me blankly. Then his eyebrows pulled together tight.

"Go," he said. He yanked me up by the arm. "Go home! I have work to do." He pushed me toward the tent door. I backed away from him. My thigh scraped against the sharp corner of the table. "Get out of here," he yelled at me. His face was red, his mouth distorted. I tugged at the hem of my shirt, then tumbled through the flaps and ran. I ran across the field, through the wet grass and into the woods where I crouched behind some trees.

It stopped raining and the sun came on hot again. Alexander went to work. I watched as he hammered, pounding hundreds of nails, filling the walls in with lumber, closing up his house.

When my mother came across the field, Alexander climbed from the ladder. She wore a light dress that ballooned in the wind, then went between her legs, clung to her body. She reached down and pulled the dress straight. Her braid fell over one shoulder and she held on to it as she talked to him. I thought she might be looking for me. And when she left, making her way back through the tall grass, Alexander watched her. He watched her, even as he went up the ladder, holding on with one hand.

In the next days, I stayed out of sight, watching Alexander work from a distance. At night I slept uneasily. I had dreams: Alexander kissing me on the lips; Alexander wincing when I began to sing. I'd come awake, momentarily unsure of the truth.

Then one night I heard my mother up and about. The spring on the screen door jingled. In the next moment, I was not far behind her on the road. I followed her to the field and watched as she passed by the dying campfire. Alexander held the tent flaps apart for her and I almost called out, but it was too late and she was inside.

There's something else that comes to mind. I don't know when it happened; I don't know where to place it. It occurred more than once. I'd heard my mother speak to my dead father. I heard her through my bedroom wall. She spoke to him and he must have answered because there were pauses and breaks—empty spaces, then she would respond. Hearing her made me feel sad; it was disturbing, but at the same time the lull of her voice had comforted me. Since Alexander's arrival, she'd grown silent. I hated his house—the white lumber, the blackened cement, the sheets of plywood. These were some of the things I thought as I hid in the grass. And some things weren't even thoughts. Some things were stones in my mouth, hard under my tongue. They were nails in my ears—those ghost words only my mother had heard.

I waited. Mosquitoes bit my ankles and scalp. Finally she left his tent, crossed the field and disappeared into the woods. The humid air settled in my lungs. I waited until the world was still; even the crickets seemed asleep. The muscles in my arms and legs grew taut, and I pulled myself to my knees. When every sense in my body was focused, I rose.

I could hear him breathing through the canvas. I could taste the canvas. I lifted the fly slowly, silently, and stepped in. It was dark, but I had my night eyes on and the moon cast enough light so I could see his shape there on the cot. I heard him, that deep breathing of sleep, filling the dank air. I touched the slope of the ceiling all the way across. I put my palm on it so I knew where I was, to guide my steps, and I touched it because I wanted to. When I came alongside the head of his cot, I could tell how his mouth was open. His chin was tilted up, his light hair spread out on the pillow. I could have shook him awake or yelled, "Boo!" But what I did was lift my hand, one finger pointed. I aimed my finger and moved it slowly. I didn't touch his lips. I did not touch his tongue. I put the tip of my finger inside his mouth. I put my finger in there, and then I took it out.

I left his tent. I crossed his site. My clothes were damp, and I was cold. The last thing I remember was the heat from his campfire rushing toward me. I don't remember walking home.

For days, especially when it rained, the stink of burnt wood wafted through the windows at night and entered my dreams. I woke in starts thinking our house was on fire. One night I slid out of a nightmare, thinking I'd smelled smoke. I got up to check around the house, and the odor disappeared the moment I threw back my sheet and put my feet on the floor. The kitchen was dark except for the glow of pilot lights on the stove. When I went down the hall toward the living room, I smelled not smoke, but perfume. The room was unlit, but I could make out my mother standing in front of the picture window. She was naked and the moonlight showed her thin figure, her slightly bowed legs, the curve of her hips and narrow waist. I didn't dare let her know I was there, nor could I take my eyes off her. The perfume stung my nose; I'd never smelled it before. For a moment it was as if I were seeing some other person, not my mother, so peculiar was the combination of fragrance and stance. When she turned, I pressed myself to the wall and she passed without knowing I was there. I felt her loneliness and I sensed that I'd contributed to it somehow. I went back to bed and stared into the dark.

2.

A FEW MONTHS PASSED; I turned thirteen. "A *teenager*," my mother exclaimed, as if it were something horrible I'd become, or done.

Though there were just the two of us living under the same roof (David won a scholarship and transferred to Northlee Academy), my mother and I rarely saw each other. I went out the back door when I heard her coming in the front. Or I waited until she left before I crept into the hall. If we ate together (which wasn't often), it was in silence, eyes down. I was afraid to look at her.

Then one early fall weekend she decided to cook a feast. The cabin was full of cooking smells. I stayed in my room despite her cheery musings through my door about what a fine meal we'd have and how I ought to set the table and use the good plates and the cloth napkins.

When she called me out, the table was already set and dishes of steaming food filled the space between our plates. At the other end of the table, where my father used to sit, there was a large bouquet of yellow sunflowers stuck in a tin bucket.

She handed me a dish of green beans. I took three. She scowled at the beans on my plate and handed me the mashed potatoes. The spoon stuck as I lifted a heavy glob, tapped most of it back into the bowl and snapped the rest onto my plate. She shook her head at me, so I dug the spoon in again and plopped another glob on top of the beans, then another. There was salad, and a platter of neatly sliced ham. There were small bowls filled with pineapple rings and her own pickled beets. There was pasta with homemade pesto. I loaded my plate. I piled it up, taking two or three helpings of everything. She ignored me and served herself.

"I thought a bouquet would cheer us up," she said. I looked at the sunflowers with their skimpy petals sticking out around their heads, like silly bonnets tied around seedless, pocked faces.

I stuck my fork into the mess on my plate and moved things around, but I couldn't eat.

"Katy," she said, after a moment and with a break in her voice. "I'm worried about you."

I snickered. It was an ugly sound, like gravel in my throat.

"I wish you'd talk to me," she said. "I miss you."

"That's a joke," I said. The words scraped the roof of my mouth. "You don't even know me, or anything about me."

"I think I do, though," she said. "We're not so different, you know."

Her braid was draped over her shoulder, the tassel end disappearing below the table. Her face had taken on the hue of health, rosy and not so drawn. She was beautiful, more and more so every day.

"Oh right," I said. "I forgot how we were joined at the hip."

"Not like *that*," she said. "Just, we've been through a lot together. And I was a girl once too, you know. I had dreams and plans."

"And then you *screwed* them all up," I said. "I'm sure Dad would be proud of you."

Her mouth was open, but she didn't speak. The confused expression on her face withered into what I thought was shame. She pushed back her chair and left the room. I listened to her footfalls going down the hall.

There were all the serving dishes of food growing cold and our untouched plates. Dessert, waiting on the side table, was her famous Carey Cobbler with her own canned peaches. I was stunned at the meanness I was capable of. The sunflowers blazed. I recalled that I'd been in the field earlier that night, watching the tent. I remembered how angry I was. Maybe I was capable of anything, of more than I'd imagined. Guilt must not store well. It grows and mutates, like mold in a jar. The jar must have been expanding over time. That night it burst.

3.

A YEAR CIRCLED AND WOVE BACK INTO SUMMER. I was fourteen.

I got a job cleaning horse stalls at the Smith Farm. My mother worked as a nurse at the local clinic in Leah. We avoided each other. Or anyway, I stayed away from her.

When I envision those years after the fire, I picture hallways full of doors. Or doors that stood unattached in fields, in forests, in the middle of rooms. I opened them to more doors. I could never get anywhere.

While working at the farm, I played a game, pretending that the next stall would open into some other world like the wardrobe in the *Narnia* chronicles. The children in those stories could go inside and live adventures for years and years while only minutes passed in the real world. The gray matter in my head was its own contained world—finite, yet infinite in the possibilities of where I could go. I sank into it. Outside, there was my body. It was in the way. I hated it. Despised the soft breasts that rose from the hard washboard under my skin.

One day I sat on a stump in the field and smoked a cigarette. The only thing still standing in the ruins was the crumbling chimney. Orange daylilies sprouted in clumps where the front door used to be. Blackberries edged in, thick and full of thorns. Poplar trees had rooted inside the hole. The field was filling in with saplings and brush, but it was still mostly low blueberry bushes and yellow grass. And there in the middle was the island—a set of stone steps, leading up to nowhere. There was nothing charred or black anymore. Everything had disintegrated or sunk into the ground. I rubbed the cigarette out on the bottom of my sandal and put the butt in my shirt pocket.

I closed my eyes and pictured my parents walking hand in hand. My mother stepped high over the grass and gathered her dress in a bunch above her knees. My father wore a T-shirt—a cigarette box rolled into the sleeve—his arm muscles bulging. *Sing "Barbara Allen" with me, Katy,* he'd say. My father was so young when he died.

When I opened my eyes I saw a man at the far corner of the field. I squinted. Alexander, walking toward me. It seemed impossible. It couldn't be him, and yet it was. He'd moved to Oregon, the other side of the country. I'd heard he got married, had some other life. My hands began to tremble. I stood up.

"Little Kate," he called out. "I can't believe it."

I felt my face turn hot and I prayed it didn't show. I thought of ice—a piece at the back of my neck. My stomach muscles tightened—something inside me stirring, perched on its haunches.

He looked just the same, now thirty. Lanky, sandy hair, fine straight nose, and tanned skin that looked tough as salted hide, like you couldn't scratch a mark in it with the sharpest fingernail. I'd changed considerably from the girl he'd known, but it wasn't hard to guess it was me.

"What are you doing here?" I said.

"Going to sell my land," he said. He smiled and there it was, the little gap between his two front teeth. A tiny space like a miniature door. Goose bumps rose on my arms. Alexander pinched his earlobe and scratched the back of his head. He had a knapsack slung over one shoulder.

"I'll never rebuild," he said. "No money. My marriage is on the rocks." I pictured a tall skinny woman, Alexander's double, sitting on a cairn. "Just finished walking my land," he said. "Got my boundaries all marked off."

"You have a buyer?" I asked. My knees were shaking. I shifted from one foot to the other.

"Appalachian Mountain Club is interested," he said. "But they don't have much money."

"They'd be good," I said. I knew that the AMC would preserve the land, keep it wild. I didn't want anyone to build close to our cabin. Maybe I never *had*. I felt dizzy.

"It's strange being here," he said. "It kind of hurts." I took out my cigarettes and knocked one loose. "How's your mother doing?" he asked. "I thought of stopping over there, but I got busy. She still on her own?"

My mother dug drainage ditches in the road and chopped wood. Her gardens flourished and she brought baskets of vegetables to all the new people on Cascom Mountain Road. She'd cut her hair short and stayed fit. She was someone I barely knew. She was on her own. I shrugged.

"Never remarried?" he said and it sounded more like a statement than question.

"No."

"Well, she's still young. Plenty of time."

I narrowed my eyes at him. "She never will," I said. I hated the sound of my voice. I felt as though I'd put a curse on her. I lit a cigarette, shook the match and tossed it on the ground.

"You shouldn't do that," he said, and I thought he meant smoke. People told me that all the time.

"I don't care," I said. "I could be hit by a truck tomorrow."

"I mean, you could start a fire," he said. He stooped and picked up the match.

My chin twitched as I took a drag, filling up my lungs.

"Still hot," he said and crumbled the match head between his fingers. He handed me the remains. I emptied the cardboard stick into my shirt pocket. He pursed his lips as if he was preparing to say something else. He stared at the pocket.

"I can't get over it," he said. "You're so grown up. Skinny." Then he pointed at my head. "Your hair," he said. "It's really long again."

A cold sweat tingled over me. I wiped at the back of my neck and tucked my hair behind my ears. After the fire I'd cut my hair short because it smelled awful and some of it was singed.

Now my body felt as though it was about to fold up on itself. My neck couldn't prop my head, my shoulders couldn't support my neck, and so on, continuing down. Alexander glanced at his foundation, then away like he couldn't bear to look at it. He sighed and dug his heel into the ground.

"I better set up before it gets dark," he said and patted his knapsack. There was a bedroll attached to it.

"You're going to camp here?" I said.

"Cheaper than a motel," he said. Then he turned and started off. He walked fast with long strides. His khakis were baggy around his legs and his shirt tail flapped. He was moving away from me, which seemed impossible because I felt as bright as a lantern in the dark. In the next second, I was following him.

Alexander struck a match and lit a little teepee of sticks I'd helped him gather for his campfire. A swirl of smoke rose from it. He put his face close to the ground and blew. A flame poked up. When the fire took hold we stepped back and gazed at it.

"Just like old times," he said, then looked away. In the dimming light you could almost imagine that the bushy clump of debris was a structure, a small house, standing alone in the field. Alexander walked over to it.

As I came up behind him, he put one foot on the stone steps, his arms outstretched as if he meant to embrace the mass of small trees that grew inside the hole.

"My house," he said.

I remembered the moonlight throwing shadows across the frame of his house. I remembered the embers still pulsing in his campfire. I'd walked past the campfire, hadn't I? Or had the force of anger—an intense gravity—dragged me back?

I shivered, wrapped my arms around myself and watched as Alexander climbed over the decayed wall and descended. I looked toward the woods, but then I took a step forward and another until I was standing on the highest stair. I looked down on the top of his head. I could see that his hair had thinned in one spot and scalp showed through. He snapped branches, clearing a space. Rocks had caved in from the sides and there were grassy humps of ground grown over beams and stones.

"Nice rec room," I said. "Where's the pool table?" He didn't laugh.

"I wanted this so much," he said. "I loved building, and this land." Then he reached up and put his hand on my foot. "Come in," he said.

The moment his fingers touched my toes it was as if I were back there in time. I could smell the ancient odor of the tent—damp and moldy, suffocating. Then suddenly I was racing forward. Memories started coming to me from impossible directions. I saw myself on stage in a concert hall, a spotlight illuminating me. Then I looked up into the ball of light, and it was the moon through a telescope. And the stars that I'd studied all my life. Then down on earth I saw an old woman, her hair in long gray braids, pinned around her head like I always thought I'd wear my hair one day. I saw myself holding a small child, and then I *was* the child, and I could see the face of my mother looking back. My heart was going too fast; I had to stop it. I slid my foot away from his fingers.

"It wasn't an accident," I said. I could tell that what I said was nothing—the words, out of context, out of time, had no meaning. "I saw her go in your tent." He looked up, his head tilted as if he were having trouble hearing me.

"You've lost me," he said.

"My *mother*," I said as if that was enough. "I saw you. I was *here*." I wanted to convey everything all at once, shape the whole world again, but it was complicated and I found myself telling him things out of sequence, and backwards: My mother talking to the wall. How she wouldn't eat. The floods, and my father's smashed truck towed behind Beaulieau's Garage. I conjured up the campfire, the coals, the heat reaching for me. Alexander was silent, probably trying to put everything in an order that made sense. Finally I said, "I burned down your house."

"No," he said, his voice soft. "Kate, you've got it wrong. You didn't do it."

"But I did!" I reached for some bushes and squeezed the twigs into my palm.

"It was spilled kerosene," he said. "My own fault. I got up to piss and tripped over the can. It must have been dripping and I wasn't thinking. I carried it with me as I went by the campfire and set it on the platform. I was taking a leak when it ignited. You didn't do it. Did you really think that? All this time, did you really think that?"

I felt as if I was rushing down dark tunnels in my brain looking for missing pieces of information, his voice following me.

"I ran up to your place to call for help," he said. "But it was too late. Too far away for the fire department. They didn't come until dawn. Remember?"

I did. Night had receded and rays of light sifted through the trees, dulling the brightness of the lowering blaze. We'd wrapped ourselves in blankets, all three of us, sitting apart. Then there were the voices of men—the firemen finally arriving. They hiked in carrying shovels and wearing their wide rubber coats.

"Hey, little girl," one of them said and knelt near me. "Are you okay?" I nodded and stared at the ground. He shook off a huge glove. It fell at my feet. Then he worked his fingers over the top of my head. "Poor kid," he said. "Hair's all burned up." During the night an ash had rocked down from the sky and landed on me. My mother had batted it out, but not before some of my hair caught in a poof, turning smooth strands to crinkles in an instant.

The firemen started digging around the foundation. My mother went to Alexander, opened her blanket and swept it around them both. I could hear the shovels slice the ground. I heard the breeze, scuffing through the grass.

"You had such a crush on me," Alexander said from below. "You spent a lot of time here."

Then I found what I was looking for, what I'd neglected to add in. "I was only twelve years old," I said. I felt wobbly on my feet. "I was just a little girl. *Twelve.*"

He looked away from me. "It was a long time ago," he said. "Forget about it."

It was as though my mind had closed itself up like a paper fan, and now it was opening, spreading out again so I could see the whole complicated design inside. I'd set a fire. I had. But only in my mind. Then I saw that all the angles and graphs of my life were askew, off, built with the wrong dimensions, calculated on faulty equations. I was on a peak with no structure below.

"It was not a long time ago," I said. I flung my arms out, letting go of the bushes. "It wasn't a long time ago at all. It was ten seconds ago. It was right now." I scrambled down the steps and ran across the field. I ran fast and when finally I stopped and looked back, I saw an amazing sight. White moths rose and circled near the campfire as bright as sparks rising into the night sky. Alexander stood near them, caught at the edge, his figure dark and floating, like a tiny lost astronaut.

Everything matters—it's all true—if you believed it, if you built on it. I turned and walked off. I left him there. I lifted my arms and flew away. I flew so far that I passed above the old, gray-haired woman. She was sitting on a stump in the middle of a field, singing with her hands pressed over her ears. When she saw me, she smiled and waved, pointed the direction I should go, because I'd traveled too far.

But I found my way back and touched down on my mother's roof.

"Ah," my mother said. She handed me a Coke and sat beside me on the warm shingles. "It's a perfect night for stargazing."

"Yes." I felt the heat of her body next to mine.

"So, how is old Alexander anyway?" she asked.

"Okay, I guess. He asked about you."

"That's nice," she said. Then she was quiet and I wondered if she was thinking about the past.

"We built a fire," I said, "and talked. Then I just wanted to get home."

"Look at all those stars," she said.

Her face was turned to the dome of night and its constellations. I felt as if we were moving, the cabin atop the land. This was my mother, forever. How could I have given up such a view? A door opened; I went through.

The Skater

AFTER CIRCLING SEVERAL TIMES, Mr. Goodman left the rink to follow the river. The surface was smooth, the ice transparent, weeds down below wavering from the bottom. Bubbles like strings of pearls hung through thicker layers. Up ahead the ice appeared gray and green and white. He wondered if Caroline would come after him. He was relieved when he looked back and she wasn't there. Then, strangely, he felt disappointed. The girl hadn't followed. She was stronger than that.

He kept going—extended strides, arms swinging side to side. The river narrowed, wove through dense woods, then passed between expanses of snow-buried field. His blades scraped out a rhythm, a determined cutting sound like knives on a whetstone—the only noise as the sky grew dim. He went on in a trance—just one more bend, one more curve. The river spoke up against the weight, groaned, shifted in its skin. Mr. Goodman stopped, pivoted, back-skated, held still. The frigid air filled his lungs as if with something solid—one last real breath.

The search party found Mr. Goodman at the elbow of the river where black water roiled up through an opening in the ice. It was a long way downstream from the hole he'd fallen through. The water surged in the bend. Bushes, heavy and coated silver, sagged from the bank where the body had lodged. The current bounced under him so his body undulated, and his skates weighted his feet, but his torso kept bobbing up as if he were just about to stand.

The men made their way down the bank through the underbrush and held a flashlight on his face. They could see that one of Mr. Goodman's eyelids was crinkled shut, as if in an exaggerated wink. The other eye was open, glazed and dark, staring at nothing. A blue-gray hue had crept up his neck.

David moved forward and slipped a half-step on the icy bank. Although his own father had died when he was twelve, he'd never actually seen a dead person before.

Mr. Levine turned and put his hand on David's chest. "Stay back, now," he said.

"I'm eighteen," David said, then felt foolish. He was a senior, older by a few months than most students and in the habit of letting people know. "I can help," he said. "It's all right."

"God," Mr. Levine said. His mouth tightened, and then he put a gloved hand over his eyes and coughed. David realized that Mr. Levine was crying.

He thought he should touch the man, a pat on the elbow, but his hand stayed where it was inside his jacket pocket. The mist of their breath was caught for a second in a beam of light, as the other men began the work of dragging Mr. Goodman out.

Mr. Levine moved down the bank. David knew that Mr. Levine and Mr. Goodman had attended the same college, then taken work at Northlee Academy. Together they coached David's soccer team.

ooooooooo

When Mr. Goodman hadn't returned to the public skating area, the wide part of the river behind the mills, when he hadn't glided with his usual flourish into the midst of the skating party, Caroline began to worry. While other students sat on the bench, laughing and unlacing their skates, Caroline gazed at the trees where the river narrowed. At one point she jumped up, saying she thought she saw Mr. Goodman, far away and small, his blue and white striped hat atop his head, but no one was there. The others left for the dining hall. They said they would report him missing. Caroline paced out to the middle of the river and back, her skates tied together and slung over her shoulder.

"Something's wrong," she said as David did a walk-slide into her. He took hold of her arm, nearly falling.

There were a few lights on in the ground floor windows of the factories on the other side. The windows were tall and bright; if someone were to skate in front of them, his silhouette would be visible. Past the old buildings a concrete bridge arched over the river. Headlights shuddered between the guardrails and lit the ice below in strobes. There was no sign of him.

Mr. Goodman struggled, reached across the ice, his fingers trying for a nub or ridge. How ridiculous, such a shallow river, yet his pedaling feet couldn't find bottom. Freezing water soaked his clothes as he lunged, slipped, dropped back. There was a moment when, mostly out, he rested, thanked God, but then the edges slickened, mouthed him in. He flailed. Dark sky, jabbing cold. Just before he lost consciousness he imagined the girl, Caroline, blurred through the water and hovering above, her small white feet dangling through the hole. He tried to grab hold, but it was like trying to grasp a reflection.

David watched the men. They had to be careful. The water was moving fast at the bottom of the bank and the footing was slippery. Chunks of ice, flat and jagged, lay like overlapping shingles, the water churning underneath. It was hard to see.

One man grabbed hold of a slender tree, stretched out with a hook, caught the collar of Mr. Goodman's jacket and jerked him closer, lost hold, tried again. David was glad Caroline had been persuaded to stay behind. It was a gruesome sight and weirdly mechanical. They pulled the body out and hauled it up the bank to the flat spot where Mr. Levine and David stood watching. One man had gone for a stretcher and when it arrived, David helped position it. The men lifted the body onto the litter, tied it down.

That night, after the body had been brought in, David showered and waited until his hall was quiet before sneaking out. When he climbed through the window Caroline had agreed to leave unlocked for him, he found the room empty. He'd never been in her room before, but it was much like his own dorm room with dark wainscoting from floor to shoulder, white walls, worn floorboards, a large sizzling radiator. He passed between the two beds, one without covers—she'd transferred mid-year and had no roommate. He knew that before coming to Northlee, she'd lived in Paris with her mother (who he gathered had a problem with alcohol), and then with her father in Greece. She'd stood on the edge of a volcano; she'd eaten octopus. She could speak Greek and French.

Growing up in New Hampshire wasn't very interesting by comparison, though when he'd told her that his father had died, she'd listened, her eyes watering. Then she said, "I miss my father, too," though her father wasn't dead, but recently remarried and living in Athens. It was similar, he guessed—an absence. "She doesn't like me much," she'd said, meaning her father's new wife. "I think that's basically why I'm here."

Now, he peeked out into the hall. At first he didn't see her, and then he heard a scuffing noise. She was at one end of the hallway near a window, pacing back and forth, her slippers sliding on the gray linoleum. For a moment he had the eerie impression that she was skating, pushing one foot forward, then the other. She wore a white T-shirt that came to her knees. He retreated a step. Then she swiveled, caught sight of him.

"David," she whispered, and came to him, took his arm, and turned him back into her room. In the dim light from a desk lamp, her hair, long, springy coils, caught reddish tones he'd never noticed before.

"It's not true," she said, as if pleading with him.

"It is, though," he said.

Her eyes filled. "I could have sworn." She pointed in the direction of the hall window. "Crossing the quad. I thought it was him."

David had taken the path between the four dorms; maybe she'd mistaken him for Mr. Goodman. After his father died his mother saw his father, but in shadowy flashes, like in the backs of strangers, moving away into crowds. She knew it wasn't him, though. Just her mind playing tricks.

"I could have sworn," Caroline said. She was trembling out of control.

He took her arm and guided her to the bed, pulled at the bedcovers. "Here. Get underneath."

"We should turn out the light," she said. "Mrs. Kimball, the dorm mother."

He switched it off and stood in the dark, not sure what to do. The radiator creaked and moaned.

"Don't go," she said. "I don't want to be alone."

He could hardly believe he was here, lying next to Caroline Lawton in bed! Two months ago when she'd enrolled after Christmas break, they'd been assigned as lab partners. They got along well, spent time studying, debating current issues, but nothing more had ever happened between them. He'd thought of kissing her, but had never dared. She was self-possessed, forthright, and in some ways her worldliness intimidated him. But there was something about her, her well-traveled life, her stories of exotic places, that inspired him, made him hopeful, as if his own life, by proximity, might open out, gain access to something larger.

He'd shucked off his jacket and toed off his boots, but wearing clothes under the comforter, he began to sweat.

She was still shaking. "Let my body heat get your blood circulating," he said, tightening his arms around her. After a while, she stopped shivering except for an occasional burst, which, when it happened, gave him permission to pull her closer, or adjust his limbs, moving her against him. Now, one of her legs draped over his, and he knew that her nightshirt must have ridden up, but he was careful not to let his hands find out. His jeans felt tight and uncomfortable. Drops ran down his sides under his shirt.

"I can't stop imagining it," she said. "It's awful."

"The thing about drowning," he tried, "is that it's probably like drifting off to sleep. Peaceful, even." Which might be true, he thought, in the final phase, but certainly not while one choked on water.

She was quiet a moment, then she asked, "Is that what happened to your father?"

He'd told her about the flash flood. How the ground, saturated from weeks of rain, couldn't absorb any more. The brook surged, taking the bridge out just as his father's truck came upon it.

"No. It was, he hit his head. Probably he was knocked unconscious, instantly."

"Did you ever see him. I mean, afterwards?" she asked, her voice low, and muffled.

"No. He was taken and cremated."

"Not like that. Like, my grandfather appeared to my mother a few days after he'd passed away. He was just standing in the kitchen, holding a teacup she'd never seen. It had little pink leaves painted around the rim. He told her not to worry, that he was okay."

"A teacup?"

"That's what she saw. That's partly how you know it's true." Before he could question this, she said, "Don't you ever wonder if maybe your father's out there somewhere, in some other state?"

"Like Kansas?" he joked. He felt her tense up, pull her leg off him. "Truthfully," he said as gently as he could, "I don't really believe in that sort of thing. I don't think there's anything after we die."

"Not like there's some lovely field and we're all angels, or anything. But maybe there's a spirit that lingers, or a presence."

Disappointment rose in his chest, but he reminded himself that she was in a fragile place, and he should comfort her. Others weren't as familiar with death as he was. He remembered when his little sister found some of their father's footprints still sunk in the mud near the back steps. *He's not gone, just invisible*, she said, and his mother had nodded as if it were true. Later, rain would wash the prints away, removing the last evidence of his father's actual weight on the ground.

"People see a lot of things," he tried, "or think they do, but that doesn't make it real."

"My mother swears by what she saw."

"Maybe it was her imagination playing tricks." Or maybe she was drunk, he thought.

"Maybe imagination isn't a trick, but a part of the truth."

"Sounds like something Mr. Goodman would say," he offered, remembering an annoying debate in English class about whether Hamlet's ghost was *real* or not.

"Oh God," Caroline cried, as if hearing Mr. Goodman's name out loud had broken a spell. "Is this just a bad dream? How can he be gone? He loved being a teacher."

"Hush," he said, and ran his hand over the top of her head. "Try not to think."

It was only a few days ago, David thought, when Mr. Goodman had sat behind his desk, leaning forward on his elbows, rolling a pen between his palms, having just called on Caroline to read out loud. Shakespeare's poetry was easy for her; the words, often stilted and awkward in other's mouths, sounded authentic in hers. When she finished she laughed, perhaps embarrassed for putting so much into it. "Very, *very* nice," Mr. Goodman had said. He looked moved, near tears. "As it should be done." Then the pen slipped from his grasp, rolled to the edge of the desk, and he grabbed for it. It flipped up and he snatched it out of the air. The class applauded and Mr. Goodman smiled, his big sideways grin, his chin raised, maybe a little surprised with himself. Then he winked at Caroline. A whole room full of students. David had felt a clench in his stomach, and he felt it again now just thinking about it.

It was just this morning when Mr. Goodman had plunked himself at the opposite end of the bench from David, and bent to unlace his boots.

Caroline was already out on the ice with the others by then. She'd been spinning, her long curls flying out under her black beret, and red mittens blinking with each turn.

"How's it going, Dave?" Mr. Goodman said, pounding a heel into his skate.

"All right," David answered. A lace had snapped and he was hunched over, trying to make a knot with fingers thick from the cold. "Crappy old skates."

Mr. Goodman finished with his own skates, stood up, and placed his boots under the bench. He crossed the snow, ankles wobbling until he stepped out on the ice, and glided forward gracefully.

Caroline started toward Mr. Goodman, her face bright and happy, but then Mr. Goodman put his hand up as if to say, "Stop," or, "Stay clear," like someone might if they were unsure of themselves on skates. But Mr. Goodman was an excellent skater. Caroline dug her blades in and shavings shot up. He said something to her, his voice low, then she went backwards, making scallops away from him. She hopped a few steps, her blades clicking, dug her toe in and pushed off. Her red mittens flew side to side. Mr. Goodman called to her, his voice stern, as if scolding a child. She twirled, toes pointed out, and stopped. Her brows tightened, and her mouth twisted down.

Then the other students, cutting circles in the center of the river, called to Mr. Goodman. He waved, and started toward them, skating away from Caroline at a wide angle. She stayed where she was, her eyes piercing the ice where Mr. Goodman had stood a moment ago.

Now, in bed, there was a slight hum in her breathing—a whimper, a high note. David moved carefully in case she was asleep, stretching out on his back as best he could in the narrow bed. He thought of ice shifting, the sound of it giving, like squishing in wet sneakers, or else a thunder crack, shooting zigzag seams away from your feet. You were supposed to lie down, expand, swim on it. There were people who, once under, survived by keeping their calm, nose elevated to the pocket of air between water and ice. You could inch along, feel for an opening. He wondered if Mr. Goodman had known that, or if he'd tried.

Now, Mr. Goodman was dead. He couldn't teach literature, or coach the team. And, David thought, he could no longer keep Caroline from him.

The current was strong. There was the weight of wet clothes and metal runners riveted to heavy boots. Liquid ice slithered between his legs, pressing the body down into mud and matted leaves and sticks. The point of one blade dug in and stuck for a moment, producing a quick cloud of silt. The arms lifted slowly. Then the body rose and bumped against the ice ceiling. There was a seeping darkness, flooding the last bits of memory with the acute sense that things were incomplete, left undone.

David woke to her face. It was startling at first—one brown eye fixed on him, the other eye hidden by his shoulder. Then she blinked, rolled onto her back and laid a hand across her forehead.

Her fingers were thin, delicate and pale. One of Mr. Goodman's hands had been encased in a dark leather glove. The other was bare, frozen into a claw. When the men hoisted the body onto the stretcher, an arm flopped out. Mr. Levine placed the arm alongside the body, and another man secured it under a cord.

It had begun to snow on the way back. Except for the sound of their muffled trudging, the men were silent. Large airy flakes floated through flashlight beams and spun around them, filling tree branches and softening edges. The snow accumulated quickly on the ground, and when they came out of the woods, the white fields glowed ahead, smooth and unbroken. If he were a kid he would have torn off, kicking up snow, free-falling backwards into it. But the men hiked on, quiet in their serious thoughts.

"I had a horrible dream," Caroline said. "I was skating and I looked down and he was under my feet, below the ice. Glaring at me."

"Just a dream," he said and patted her shoulder, and let his hand rest there. A door banged somewhere, and he flinched. Voices in the hallways—girls getting up.

"You'd better go," she whispered.

"I'll see you in homeroom," he told her, as he moved to the edge of the bed and slid his feet into his boots. "Mr. Levine said there won't be any classes, but they want to make sure everyone knows. Squelch rumors, that sort of thing."

"Rumors?" she said, her voice shrill.

"You know, like if it was suicide."

"Oh, God!" She flung the covers back, startling him.

"It's just some people were saying that," he said. "Because he was someone who'd know better. But, also, they were talking about the ice. You know, how it's deceptive this time of year with all the freezing and thawing. It never gets thick enough, or something. Especially where it's fast water. It's dangerous."

"I should have gone after him!"

"What?" he said. "No you shouldn't have. The ice wasn't safe. If you'd gone up there you might have fallen through, too."

She stared at him, but it was as if she didn't register he was there. Was she angry with him? He wanted to say the right things.

"It was an accident," he assured her. "It's very sad. He was a good man." He realized instantly that he'd made a pun of the name, but she didn't appear to notice. "A brilliant teacher." The cold sheen in her eyes dissolved, turned liquid; his small tribute had weakened her.

Chunks of ice broke and fell through the grate as he stepped out onto the fire escape. He watched the ice drop to the ground below, gripped the rail, and took the narrow stairs.

"Come back tonight," she whispered.

"Of course," he said, trying to hide the excitement that shot through him. He felt like Romeo, sneaking down from the balcony.

At the bottom the snow was tracked with his own boot prints. He scuffed the snow to cover them. Then he hurried across the alley, imagining Caroline's face, high up in the dorm window and close to the frosted glass, watching him until he slipped around the corner and out of sight.

The loose glove scuttled along the river bottom until a current spun it into a slow cartwheel. It snagged momentarily in a nest of branches, then drifted past a tire, a beer can, a child's sneaker. Not far behind, the body floated, face-up under the ice, legs and arms slack. A dead eye saw nothing. The mouth hung open, allowing water freely to the lungs. Cells continued to freeze.

In homeroom David took a seat in the back near the windows. Mr. Levine arrived and sat on the edge of the front desk. He made a sad face at David. David nodded.

The hall was busy with students talking. Word had spread. Mr. Levine waited as others filed in and took their seats.

The corridor emptied. Caroline had not shown up.

"Most of you know already," Mr. Levine began, and the room settled. "But for those who might not, there's been a terrible tragedy." The last voices hushed and he continued. "Mr. Goodman is—" He took a handkerchief from his inside pocket and touched it to his mouth. "Accidentally drowned," he said. "Fell through the ice. Yesterday. Skating." He paused, the composure in his face crumbling for a second. Several students moaned.

"Parents are being notified," he went on. "But you should call them, let them know how you are."

David hadn't thought about his mother; he wished she didn't have to know. Even though it'd been six years, she didn't need any reminders of the night his father had been killed. His mother had run outside, calling his father's name, and Jeff Driver had gone after her, dragged her back inside. David had never particularly liked Jeff to begin with, and then seeing his forearm around his mother's chest, restraining her. And just the plain fact of him, standing there alive when his father was dead, was too much. Before David knew what he was doing, he slugged Jeff in the shoulder, and his little sister said, *What's happening?* as if she'd just come awake, but couldn't yet tell the difference.

Someone began to cry—Laurie in the first row. Mr. Levine slipped off the desk and stood in front of her.

"We need to be strong," Mr. Levine said. "For his son. And Rani, his wife. This won't be easy for them."

David had seen Rani, Mr. Goodman's wife, at various functions. She was slenderand pretty, and wore a single, dark braid. She was always poised with a pleasant smile.

"I've known Nick . . . I mean, Mr. Goodman," Mr. Levine said, as if the informality of using his friend's first name was a mistake. It did sound funny. Nick—a boy's name. "I've known Mr. Goodman and his wife since college, he continued. "They were childhood—"

Mr. Levine stopped suddenly, distracted, his attention drawn to the window. It was Caroline, running across the snowy plaza, black beret, and long hair swinging across the back of her down jacket. She turned the corner and disappeared around the side of the building. It seemed she'd come up from the river, but David wasn't sure.

Mr. Levine stood, chin raised, lips screwed to one side, scrutinizing Caroline's path.

"Poor Caroline," Laurie said, and David realized how everyone knew Caroline idolized Mr. Goodman. Or, he thought darkly, how she was Mr. Goodman's favorite—the teacher's pet.

"I'll miss him, *too*," another girl said, too eagerly.

"We're all suffering," Mr. Levine said to her, though his eyes hadn't left the window.

Late afternoon, a large framed photograph of Mr. Goodman, neatly combed and dressed as if for a wedding, appeared propped up on the front step of the main hall. Flowers had been laid in piles in a circle around it. Someone had left a soccer ball, held in place by a fence of stems. There was Mr. Goodman's face—his rugged good looks, the square jaw, toughened skin, and crinkles around his eyes from years of snow and sun and wind. The familiar grin weighted to the left, giving him a self-satisfied sort of look. David caught himself making the same expression as he studied the photo. Then he put his hand over his mouth and chin and pulled it away.

There were groups of students huddled together. And girls sobbing. There were students who hadn't even had a class with Mr. Goodman, claiming him in their memories.

"You okay, man?"

David turned around to find Robbie, a teammate, standing behind him.

"Yeah," David said. "You?"

Robbie nodded, but his chin dimpled, and he wiped his nose with the back of his arm. The sun, vague behind a gauze all day, was lowering, and the cold was coming on hard.

"Sucks," Robbie said, his voice teetering toward a sob.

It was sad Mr. Goodman had died, yet David couldn't feel anything—no tears, no particular sadness. He couldn't conjure up any time in the future where it might hit him—even on the soccer field—and he'd feel a loss. This bothered him slightly, but he figured, with a flicker of superiority, that he'd been through it before. He'd had to tough it out when his mother became anorexic, barely able to function. He'd watched after his little sister when they were shuffled off to live with their crazy grandmother for a while. He was only a kid then, but he'd felt older, doing what was necessary, keeping things from falling apart. It was as if he'd sped past that dark time in their lives and never looked back. Though, occasionally, he'd caught himself imagining his father coming home. Like in soap operas, his father would have forgotten who he was for a time, maybe woken up downstream somewhere, cold, disoriented, trudged across the fields, come to a farmhouse where another family took him in, and he lived as someone else, until one day when . . . But David would stop there, disgusted with himself for entertaining such a useless fantasy.

It was freezing outside and David's cheeks felt as thin as paper as he made his way up the fire escape. He couldn't wait to get inside, but when he climbed through the window he found her with her jacket on. She was pale, the color drawn out of her, except for gray half-moons that sank into the skin under her eyes. Her hair bushed out, uncombed. It scared him a little, but he was glad to be here in the warm room, the covers of the bed flung back as if asking them to return to it.

Then she said, "I have to go out."

"Out?" he said. "It's below zero."

She pulled on mittens and marched to the window, climbed through.

They walked fast across campus. The air was stiff, and their boots squeaked on the hard snow.

"We saw you this morning crossing the quad," he told her.

"I know," she said. "Mr. Levine sent Mrs. Kimball to check on me."

He thought they were heading to the river, but then she veered another way, toward a tracked path through the woods—a shortcut to the next street where the Goodmans lived.

"Mrs. Kimball told me not to," Caroline said, "but she's wrong. I need to speak to his wife."

"Please," he said, feeling sick. What did she have to say to Rani Goodman? "Let's not go there." He stopped walking, but she continued on ahead. He realized she'd worn her backpack for some reason. "Listen," he said, catching up. "I heard she collapsed when she found out."

Caroline stumbled as if his words had gotten under her feet, but went on, faster, more determined.

He wasn't sure if it was a rumor he'd heard, but he had a picture of Rani Goodman in his mind, her long dark braid draped over her shoulder, hands gripping it like a rope. The coroner pulling the sheet from the face. The one open eye; the other shut in a frozen wink. Maybe she looked toward Mr. Levine and said, "It's not him," before her knees gave.

The lights in the Goodmans' house shone out from the porch and they could see into rooms. Mr. Levine and Rani Goodman, her head lowered, passed by the window inside. They were followed by another woman, Mr. Levine's wife. Caroline started down the walkway.

"Wait," David said, but Caroline continued on.

Then, a voice from the porch, "Who are you?"

It was a boy, maybe six or seven years old, bundled up, a scarf wrapped several times around his neck and a hood pulled tight around his face.

"Oh," Caroline said. She had one foot on the porch and one on the step; her hand had flown to her chest. Then she said, "You might not remember us, Nicky, but we know who you are."

"My dad's not here," the boy said. "He died."

David felt as if he'd been punched. The boy could have been him. *My father's truck was washed off the bridge. He's dead.*

He re-membered his own casual delivery of that information, even perhaps a sense of pride—suddenly popular, the center of attention. But now, standing in front of this little boy, a swell in his throat.

"Levines are here," the boy said. "You know them?"

Caroline hoisted her pack, her thumbs under the straps.

"What are you doing out here, Nicky?" David asked. "It's cold."

"I was in the fort," the boy said, and pointed toward the yard where there was a high snow bank. A dark arch near the bottom showed the entrance. "My dad and I made it."

David had built forts like that, and he remembered now that his father had shown him how to use cardboard boxes to haul snow back out the tunnels.

"It looks like a good one," David said.

"Yes," Nicky said. "It's good." His voice sounded matter-of-fact, but his mouth tightened into a quivery pout.

David pictured how the fort would eventually melt, the arches and ceilings turning silky, dripping, then the tunnels collapsing, dangerous to be inside.

Caroline was silent. David thought for a second she'd decided not to go forward, but then she threw one shoulder back and swung the pack around, dropped it at her feet. She fumbled with the buckles, her mittens clumsy on her hands. Nicky stepped closer. David couldn't imagine what was inside and he thought he ought to snatch the bag away, but now she reached in and pulled out a boot. It was Mr. Goodman's boot. And then she drew out the other one and stood them side by side.

"He left them under the bench," Caroline told Nicky.

Nicky picked up one of the heavy boots and held it to his chest. He wrapped his arms around it and put his face into the opening as if to look for his father. He crouched, picked up the other one, turned away, and awkwardly opened the front door. Light and voices trailed out and he went inside with the boots, glanced back at them, and shut the door.

He had hoped they'd return to her room, but now they stood next to the river. Snow came down, visible inside the shafts of light that swept from the cars on the bridge. The factory windows were murky in the distance.

When they stepped out, the ice responded with a muffled cracking noise, but distant, far away from where they stood, as if the pressure here had upset the equilibrium somewhere else. They moved with caution, sliding their feet, because the new snow made it slick. It was strange to think they were on top of an abyss, a moving force, and the only thing between them and it was this fragile, changeable layer.

She stopped in the middle, and gazed upriver. If she planned to go there, he wouldn't let her.

"He's here," she said. "I feel him."

A chill drew David's shoulders up. He peered into the dark and falling snow. He saw nothing.

Needles hit his face, sleet now mixing with snow, and it occurred to him what a difference a few degrees could make between ice and water. Everything was a matter of degrees. What was real or imagined.

A car rumbled onto the bridge. Headlights flashed, panning the frozen river, and he saw how the surface stretched away from him, a smooth, white-covered field, until it met with the dark, and fell to the shadows beneath the bridge.

"I'm sorry," she said, turning toward him. "This must be awful for you. It must make you think about your father."

He felt queasy, disoriented, as if a drug had entered his bloodstream. His feet went into a slip-slide. He grabbed for Caroline's arm, but he went down hard. He lay on his back, the wind knocked out of him.

Caroline appeared above, hair hanging down.

"David? Are you hurt?"

The words were stuck inside him.

When at last they came, it was like rising to the surface, finding air.

Jupiter Shining, North of the Moon

THE SUMMER WE WENT TO A LOT OF PARTIES and stood on balconies and porches talking and drinking beer, and holding cool bottles to our foreheads because it was so hot. Hotter, they said, than it had been in ten years. We leaned on railings while insects swarmed and tapped the outside lamps above our heads. If a breeze found its way, rattling over the Iowa corn or coming up from the river, we lifted our chins and shut our eyes, savoring the moment it cooled us. Mostly the air was dead still—thick as water—making our foreheads shine. Women lifted the hair off the backs of their necks and twisted temporary buns that soon unraveled and spilled out. Men caught glimpses of bras or flesh at edges of sleeveless blouses and used the tails of their shirts to wipe their faces.

We talked about school, but mostly we talked about nothing. About love. The sounds of the party—laughter, bottle caps snapping off, the drone of voices, screen doors creaking open and bouncing shut, chairs dragged across rough boards, shouts and hoots rising and falling from this group or that—became like music, a familiar, undulating refrain. All the parties might have been the same, each blending into the other. Nothing much ever happened, until the night we lost Mira.

It was the night of Joe's party and just about everyone we could think of came out. The house sat at the edge of town—a good place for a party—far enough away from neighbors, but not out of walking distance. No one would have to drive—everyone would drink a lot. The party was subdued at first, perhaps because of the heat, until more and more people arrived, crowding the kitchen and hovering near the whirring fans in the small rooms, or filling the porch—every step down to the yard occupied.

Some preferred the fringes and stretched out in the grass by the river, batting mosquitoes and staring up at the night sky. We could trace the lines of the big dipper. Jupiter was shining north of the moon. The blackness seemed to bulge between the stars like rolling hills. The man in the moon looked upset, with hollowed eyes, or then he looked like a woman with puckered lips. Or else the face wasn't clear at all—the shadows and contours of craters could not be made into any face no matter how long we looked.

That night the moon would be full for the second time in the month. A blue moon. Only once every three years. We pondered that—what it meant—if it meant anything. Someone said he didn't believe astronauts had really walked on the moon. A government hoax. Others groaned. Cicadas motored in the trees.

Joe came down and stood over the bodies, took a sip of his beer and looked out at the river. The water picked up pieces of silver from the moon. Light from houses and lamps on the other shore glimmered on the dark surface. He followed a wavering beam across the water and squinted until it spread out in rays. When he blinked the pins of light shot back to the center and disappeared. The beer, though growing warm in his hands, tasted good and he drank the last of it in one long swallow. He held the empty bottle to his cheek; the glass was sticky. He rolled the bottle over his mouth and pressed his lips against it. We all looked at Joe when he sighed.

Joe was in love with Kate, who hadn't yet arrived at the party, and might not. We knew she was seeing some guy—a doctor we didn't know, though we'd already decided we didn't like him, because we loved Joe and wished for his happiness.

Wishing never made anything so and it was Mira who now said, "It's bad luck to wish on the moon."

It was just a mass of rock, held prisoner by the earth, and pulling tides, yet suddenly it seemed a hot eye upon us, daring anyone to ask it for anything.

Joe laughed. "I wish the moon would fuck itself," he said.

Later that night we'd have to carry Joe, near drowned, back to his room. We'd undress him and hold him in the shower until he was washed clean of mud and river grass. It would be Mira who'd sleep on the floor next to Joe's bed, reaching up every now and then to touch his wrist, feel his pulse, which was always there—a soft tick under her fingertips—and she'd imagine that his hand might awaken and settle upon her. Once she got on her knees and stared at his sleeping face—his slightly parted lips—and listened for his breath. She bent close, found the pulse in his neck and imagined kissing him there, feeling that tiny heartbeat bounce against her lips, though she never did this. He lay only a foot away from her. He breathed the same air. Through the floor she heard music turned low. Love—it was like music, like listening to Bach—which always made Mira feel a pull in the gut, up under her heart. But why? Music was just notes upon notes. Notes sliding into other notes, lingering or vanishing. Water to vapor. If only there were a spell to awaken one heart to another.

There were no spells. We knew that. You could never make someone feel something he didn't feel. Hardly anyone loved the right person. Even Kate, walking across town on her way to Joe's party, could tell you the doctor was not right for her. The streets were quiet, the pavement lit in gray pools under lampposts. The hard leather heels she'd chosen clacked on the sidewalk and echoed off dark houses. She felt as if she were the only one awake and making noise on the planet. She wondered where the doctor was and what he was doing. Perhaps he was making love to his wife.

What had brought Kate and the doctor together was a set of coincidences that she'd considered to be fate—an outside force—something mystical. They'd struck up a conversation in line at the DMV. It turned out he'd gone to a boys' camp in New Hampshire when he was a kid, and even climbed Kate's beloved Mount Cascom. They drove identical cars (1990 Hondas) of the same color (charcoal). Later, after their fingers had laced together and they'd watched their two hands caress and slide apart and around each other as if sculpting shadow images, and after she'd tasted the inside of his mouth and said, "No, we should stop. You're married," but couldn't stop, they'd find other parallels in their lives that only helped to fuel her belief (they shared the same birthday, though he was nine years her senior; both had lived on Maple Streets when they were children, though in different states). Fate.

Then, the other day, she and Mira had been seated only two tables away from the doctor and his wife at a restaurant. He would not catch her eye. The wife, a slender, attractive woman, peeled a shrimp and held it to the doctor's mouth. He opened his mouth and the wife put the shrimp on his tongue—her fingertips inside his mouth. Kate looked down at her plate. The piece of bread she'd just taken a bite of went dry, became impossible to swallow, and she had to hold it against the roof of her mouth for a long time. Only two nights before, they'd stood in the shower and his hands had traveled over her body, washing her, making lather on her stomach, down her legs. Now his hands held fork and knife. His body leaned toward the wife. Kate watched him as if through a window—his figure distorted by the warp in glass. The wife spoke, though Kate couldn't hear what she said. There was kindness in her face—chin pulled back slightly, lowered—as she listened to her husband's reply. She nodded and a fan of honey hair fell forward like a wing. When she flicked it back over her shoulder, Kate was envious at how easily the woman could possess and dismiss something so lovely as that hair.

"She's beautiful," Kate whispered to Mira. Mira nodded and they sat silently for a while. Then Kate would tell Mira that she felt as though the doctor had climbed inside her and she was seeing with his eyes, seeing the woman whose mouth, whose hands, knew him so well. Whose soft eyes held him when he sank inside her. "It's almost as if I love her too," Kate said. "I love all that he loves."

"I don't think she'd see you in quite the same way," Mira said.

Now, turning the corner and crossing to Joe's street, Kate thought about how Mira's remark had made her turn and look hard at herself. It sickened her to think she'd participated in such deceit. She could not do this to the wife. She would not be with him anymore. Adultery. A sin. "Forgive me," she said gazing up at the sky, at the bright, full moon. A dog barked on a nearby porch, startling her, and her heels tapped out a quick beat. Drinking a lot seemed like a really good idea.

ooooooooo

Before Joe, drunker than we'd ever seen him, disappeared, we would head back up to the house for more beer. On the porch, leaning against the rail, some voices were louder, maybe more serious, breaking through the din.

Mira listened to McColly talk about the man he was in love with. This man had given McColly reason to believe he cared, then broken it off. Mira offered up advice and anecdotes and like stories for McColly to reflect on. She told him about a man she'd gone out with in Austin. The guy was always pushing her away, then drawing her back. He didn't know what he wanted. One minute she'd be convinced it was over, and then he'd be at her doorstep saying he missed her. Part of her decision to come to the Midwest for school was to get away from him—to break the cycle. "Don't let Stephen do that to you," she said. She and Kate had talked about this—how sometimes you just had to accept that a person was who he was. You couldn't change him, nor could you decide that there was something wrong with yourself. Poor McColly. Mira wanted to be supportive even though everyone knew that Stephen slept with anything with two legs. No one thought Stephen was any good for him.

"He doesn't want me," McColly said. "I can rationalize that, but how do I just shut my feelings off?"

McColly was a slender man with thick gray curls, which made him look older until you saw the smooth skin of his still young face. He spoke with soft, lulling tones. He was the sort of person Mira could imagine curling up with in the afternoon. She thought it would be nice to fall asleep with McColly's voice in her ears.

ooooooooo

Though we all knew Mira was in love with Joe, she hardly ever talked about it. She'd tried to talk to Kate occasionally, but Kate was uncomfortable with the subject, given Joe's affections for her. McColly knew some things: One night, long before Kate, Joe had driven Mira home and held her in his arms, kissed her.

Sometimes Mira spoke in generalities: "If you really love someone, do you want his happiness or your own?" but we knew she was referring to herself—about how much she loved Joe. We all knew. Joe too, though he didn't want to believe it.

Only Mira noticed Joe had disappeared from the porch and she went inside to look for him, leaving McColly to gaze up at Jupiter and swear to God he'd never let himself be so vulnerable again. He'd never confess his love before the other did, or at least until he was sure of it. If one had to play games, then so be it. He'd play. He'd hide how he felt. But oh, he was so tired of it. Completely sick of it. There had to be an adult, mature, grown-up man who could meet him halfway without all this other business. There were lovers in the world, happy to be with each other. People *did* manage to do it.

"Why is this always happening to me?" McColly said.

"We want what we can't have," someone said.

"Why?" McColly said. "Why *is* that?"

Kate came up the stairs, making those sitting on the steps lean to the side to let her through. She swung a bottle of red wine by the neck.

"I think God isn't in love with me any more," she said.

"The doctor," McColly said, "isn't God."

Kate leaned into McColly's shoulder and kissed his cheek. "Open this for me, will you?" she said, and handed him the bottle.

"Has anyone seen Joe?" Mira asked through the screen door.

We all scanned the crowd and shook our heads.

We hadn't noticed when Joe opened a bottle of Beam and slipped out the back door. As he walked he took swigs. The bourbon burned pleasantly as it went down. His legs weren't working properly, his balance was off. He wasn't moving in a straight line and this made him happy. He went with it, zigzagging, stumbling. He was making his way toward the bank of the river. His boots scuffed the ground heavily.

"Thunk, thunk, thunk," he sang out loud to the rhythm of his footfalls. "Where's Kate, I need Kate, I'm drunk, drunk, drunk." He laughed and slipped, landed on one knee, gulped some whiskey, then wobbled to his feet again. He liked being drunk, his mind numbed, though it made him want Kate all the more. Right this minute. He could imagine sliding his hands around her waist, his palms finding that place where her hips began to curve. It was where he liked to hold her. That indentation of her waist, that middle of her body. He remembered opening Kate's blouse, turning each button through, and smoothing the material away until her breasts fell free.

Once, making love, he'd whispered in her ear, "I want you to let go with me." She'd responded by lifting her hips to him. She'd dug her fingers into his back, pulling him as if she couldn't get close enough to him. Now he wondered if she'd only been acting. It seemed impossible. If she were acting, how could he love her?

The river moved along silently, following the curve of its low bank. He smelled the humid, swampy odor of tall grasses growing in the shallows. The surface shone with flat planes of brown, or gray, or olive. Some areas were pricked with sparks of yellow, or white. The water was not just black, though his mind kept asking him to see it that way—to understand it as only dark water. Strange to think that one's vision could be trained to be so inaccurate. Brainwashed. Brains washed and dulled. Love conquers all. Love is blind. Love hears no voice but its own. All's fair. True love—an oxymoron.

He chuckled and swung the bottle up to his mouth. Kate. Kate. Kate. Just a name, a word. But her—her laugh. He did love her.

Later, long after Mira was gone, we'd remember how she searched the house for Joe. She reminded us of moonlight—fair and wispy and floating from room to room, passing between people, asking if they'd seen him. We'd give each other looks as she moved on. We'd watch her climb the stairs, disappearing little by little behind the banisters, until her white calves and bare feet flashed away.

At the top of the stairs Mira leaned into Joe's bedroom door and flicked on the light. There was his unmade bed, his desk covered with papers, a chair full of clothes, a sneaker on the windowsill. The other sneaker lay on its side at the foot of the bed. It was bad luck to leave shoes separated from one another and Mira could not resist entering the room to align them. At the window she paused and looked down on the yard. She saw people standing at the base of the porch steps and some further out on the lawn. She watched Kate cross to a group carrying her bottle of wine and someone hold his cup out for her to fill. Then Kate turned back toward the porch, her long blond braid swinging behind her. Her face was bright and she was smiling at someone, probably McColly, and Mira was glad to see her friend so cheerful. But then, in just the second before Kate went up the steps and out of view, Mira saw something else cross Kate's face—a tightening of the mouth and a look to the side—the pain of which spun into Mira and made her own chest heave, a quick intake of breath. That Kate could not see herself—her beauty, her sweetness—and that she would waste her love on someone who did not love her, made Mira shiver with anger.

Mira placed Joe's sneakers side by side on the floor at the foot of his bed. The canvas was worn at the toes and puckered from the shape of Joe's feet as if he stood in them now.

"Despite everything," McColly said. "I keep hoping Stephen will change his mind."

Kate sipped her wine. "You can't shake hope," she said. "She comes up behind you, drapes herself over your shoulders and hangs on. Damn her to hell."

"We would all kill ourselves if not for hope," McColly said. "And what makes you think Hope is a she?"

Kate shrugged. "Grief is definitely male," she said. "Wearing black. Or like a shadow that can step inside your body."

"What's Love, then?" someone asked. "Male or female?"

"Bisexual," McColly said. "Maybe a guy in drag."

"So Love *is* male," Kate said. "He has a penis?"

"It would be a help," McColly said.

When McColly first noticed Stephen, he thought he would never in a million years be attracted to such a person. The man was totally macho, muscles and skintight jeans. He strutted around the dance floor. He even had a box of cigarettes rolled up in his T-shirt sleeve, bulging above his overworked arm. Stephen's earrings (three in one ear) caught light—golden droplets. The man was positively full of himself. There was no rational explanation for McColly's attraction; still, he was smitten.

"It's Stephen's loss," Mira had said. "The guy is a fool to let you go."

"Are those fireflies," Kate said to McColly now. They leaned close together, gazing out at the dark field. Tiny orbs blinked on and off. Stars on the ground. A mirror of the sky.

"You know why they flash like that?" McColly said. "They're trying to get laid."

The music up at the house rose and flattened as if riding through the air on waves of heat. Joe sat down in the grass. Kate had told him things: "I didn't know he was married until it was too late." No ring, she'd said. He didn't wear a ring. She'd looked for one. If she'd known, would that have stopped her, stopped love? The bastard.

"He's not a cruel person," she'd said. "Not evil. I can't believe that about him. It's just something that happened." Kate was naked underneath Joe. She was looking into his eyes. "I thought maybe I would get over him. I want to. But I can't. The last thing in the world I want to do is hurt you."

He could smell her hair—a soft, shampoo smell. Her legs were between his. They'd just made love. Her hands had caressed and dug and asked and pleaded for more and told stories and lied. Lied.

"I could love you, Kate," Joe had said. "No secrets. Real love." He didn't know if this were true. He just knew he couldn't possibly let her go. He could not let this person, this woman who lay naked in his arms, leave him. Could not let her make what had just happened meaningless.

They made love again. Then she left. Making love was nothing to her.

Nothing.

We couldn't have imagined Joe would have gone so far—would have stepped into the river, felt the water swallow his shoes, soak the hem of his shorts. The grass wrapped around his ankles as he sloshed through the muck. There was the moonlight wavering atop the surface. Blue moonlight. He wanted to step into it, let it travel up his body, wash over his face, but it kept sliding away. He tried to run after it, bottle still in his fist. Then he fell over. The water pulled him down. It filled his ears. Muffled the world. He rolled, his feet searching for the bottom. He clawed the water and tried to push off weeds that gave and slithered through his fingers like hair.

McColly watched as Kate balanced her wineglass on the rail, then lifted herself up and sat. "Don't you dare fall off," he told her.

"Have the fireflies stopped blinking?" she asked, peering out at the field. Only an occasional pulse of light appeared.

"Insects have better luck than us," McColly said.

"Live a day," Mira said, coming up. "Mate, then die."

"Did you find Joe?" McColly asked.

"He's not anywhere," she said.

When we found Joe he was face down in the water. He couldn't have been submerged long. We rolled him over and he coughed and choked, and we dragged him ashore and stuck our fingers in his mouth and turned him on his side. He spit water and laughed and asked where his Beam was.

"God, Joe," Kate said. "Jesus Christ. That was fucking stupid." She held his head in her lap. She was crying.

"Kate?" Joe said. "You came to my party?"

We'd all come to the party looking for love. There were some couples and we watched them with envy, with interest, with pity. Those couples had left early. The rest stayed—stood in a circle outside on the lawn, unable to leave, not ready to leave. No one dared to break away.

It would be Mira who'd sleep on Joe's floor, next to his bed. At one point she'd stand and cross to the window. There was a breeze coming through the screen and she let it lift her hair and flutter her blouse. Joe rolled on his side and she listened for the rhythm of his breathing to return, smooth and even. Joe's sneakers lay on the floor where she'd left them earlier. She stepped forward and slid her feet into them. They were way too large. She could hear the soft voices of those still in the yard and she wondered if Kate was still there.

It had been Kate who'd suggested they go down to the river to look for Joe. "Let's go find our Joe," she said. She and Mira held hands. They skipped across the grass, swinging their arms high. Their skirts filled and twirled. McColly ran up behind and separated them. They put their arms around him and the three walked together.

Everyone was laughing and calling Joe's name as they got close to the river. All of them were giddy and drunk and full of moonlight, as they branched out, swept the area. Mira moved with Kate. They went side by side, along the bank, not yet fearful, still sure they'd find him asleep in the grass. Mira felt heat, as if it were a tangible body, walking between the two of them. She reached for Kate's hand again, but this time Kate would not take hold and their fingers slid apart.

"Where *is* he?" Kate said, her voice full of worry. Then, just before they caught sight of Joe, his white T-shirt swollen with air above the surface, and just before Kate screamed and splashed her way to him, Mira realized that in that hesitation—that undone grasp—love had rearranged itself between them all.

Mira stepped out of Joe's sneakers and knelt next to the bed. She stared at his sleeping face—his slightly parted lips. Our Joe, she thought. How was it that love could be so confused? So misdirected? Lovers all facing the wrong way. Yet love was boundless among them. It saw itself in every other. If one had the power to turn from it. To remove oneself. Tear oneself from its gravity, might it spin out in another direction? Might it shift and turn and envelop those who waited, hearts open? Mira would step out of the way. In hope, with hope, that love would enter in.

Mira left us. Vanished. Water to vapor. She wandered into the corn field. She evaporated. She disappeared. Our Mira. Had we ever really known her? She was gone, but not invisible. We'd talk about her. A piece of music might remind us of her and we'd feel a pull inside, up under our hearts.

That summer scientists would find evidence of life on early Mars. One of Jupiter's moons, too. We'd learn that the blue moon had come full as June turned to July, and July would have its own full moon. Hence, two blue moons—one after another—in the same year. Anything was possible. Nothing definite.

"She went back to Texas," McColly suggested. "Her *lone*-star state."

"When I write to her," Kate said. "I'll tell her she's our new favorite topic of conversation."

"In my room that night," Joe would say. "I dreamed I'd drowned. It wasn't so bad, really. Pleasant. I could see up through the surface of the water to the moon. Then all sorts of hands reached down for me. Mira's face was the only one that came clear."

We all shrugged and shook our heads.

And that night, the night of the party, afterwards we'd walked down the dark streets and up the hill, where we stopped because a streetlight had just dimmed as we came under it. We said it was magic. Cosmic. We thought we had powers—our own brightness had caused it to turn out.

We moved on, talking about the party—what happened. About love. How Joe had nearly died for it. Then, at the corner, we walked backwards, saying good-bye, and went our separate ways.

The Man from Nothing

THAT DAY THE RIVER GREW WIDE AND SLOW as it wove through dense wilderness. Kate looked over the edge of the canoe at the surface of the water—a mirror of the sky. Clouds, their edges blurred and seeping, floated deep inside the reflection and the dark hills fell vividly into the depths. If she looked too long, it made her dizzy, as if she were being pulled into that other world.

Thomas's paddle dipped and dribbled behind her. They'd been on the river for three days; in three more they'd reach the bay. Her shoulders were sore and sunburned, and her knees were bruised and tarnished gray from kneeling on the bottom of the canoe.

She saw the image of a bird—a fleck of white—flying as if entrapped within the water, and she looked up in time to catch a seagull going overhead. She watched until it disappeared and once more an ache sucked her down. Grief. When she was a child, grief was green—similar sound and letters. And also because her father had died when she was young, and he'd died in the spring just as the new leaves twisted open on the trees. Now, as she shut her eyes and felt the resistance of the water against the blade of her paddle, she saw grief as a cupped palm, trying to hold something that was no longer there. Six months ago their four-year-old son had been killed in a fall from the roof of the house.

Before Tommy—little T, they called him—was born, Kate and Thomas had done lots of canoe trips, so returning to the river was a way of going back in time to before anything had happened. But it wasn't like starting at the beginning again at all. Their son had lived and died. You could not erase it. For brief moments one could forget; sometimes she woke in the mornings, her mind blank until a dark awareness crept through her, and she had to realize it was true all over again.

"We should look for a place to camp," Thomas said from the stern.

Kate scanned the shore. It could be any spot, but preferably one where it wouldn't be hard to drag the canoe out. Also where there might be a clearing, but the forest was dense. She liked being on the river, headed in one direction, each day's purpose the same—to go forward. Yesterday they'd drifted over a car. It appeared suddenly just beneath the surface, lying on its side. Hulking, bluish metal. The fender, still silver and gleaming, corkscrewed from the front end. Her hands went weak and she almost lost hold of her paddle. The car's door hung open like a wing, revealing the steering wheel and the seamed upholstery—so eerie and wrong. Thomas saw the car too, one second later, and lifted his paddle as the canoe slid silently, swiftly over and away. Around the bend there were more junked vehicles, pushed down the steep bank, half-slid into the stream and under water.

"Nice place for a parking lot," Thomas had said.

Usually it was rocks or submerged trees that hid just under the murky surface and suddenly scraped along the bottom of the canoe. Since the cars, every twirl or swell set her on edge, but it was her job to watch, to spot and inform. When the water was deep, she felt calmer. Nothing to see below—just the reflection painted over the surface—*into* the surface because it did not look flat and she couldn't make her eyes see it that way—the illusion of dimension was so convincing.

"I think there are falls near the Indian reservation," Thomas said. "We should get off before then. I'm too tired to carry anything."

That morning they'd portaged around a large dam. They'd pulled out a good ways before the embankment since it was a working dam with signs posted along the hill warning them as they drew near. They could see the glassy ridge where the water dropped off between the gates and the area called the point of no return, where the current was too powerful to back-paddle against. They'd hauled the canoe ashore, stowed it in the grass, and carried the supplies first. It was a long bushwhack through prickers and scrub around the machinery of the dam, then down a hill and farther, to where the water, having made its roaring plummet, spun out and became smooth again. Then they went back, hoisted the canoe aloft, and walked with their heads inside it. They hiked awkwardly, Thomas trying to match her stride; even on land she was in the bow and went first.

Most dams were small enough so they could get out and pass the canoe hand over hand. In rocky shallows they waded, taking the canoe by its gunwales, maneuvering it between rocks and over smooth aprons of granite until the water was deep enough to take their weight again. They'd shot through rapids, skidded into sluices, the canoe pivoting, then plunging, bow first, clunking and swiveling between boulders. There were dents now—some long and pencil thin, some larger, blasted indentations in the aluminum. Thomas examined these marks, turning the canoe over for the night.

They'd never canoed the Penobscot. They'd done other rivers in Maine and New Hampshire: the Saco and the Allagash and some day trips on smaller streams, all before their son was born. For two years they'd lived together unmarried until she got pregnant. She felt differently after marriage—better, at ease. Thomas did too. *It feels safe,* he said. She'd wondered about that—how documentation, a license, and those quick vows gave the illusion of a safer haven, but it did. The baby grew and she looked at this man who was now her husband, unable to remember who she was or how she'd existed before him. His skin was her skin. When he broke his wrist in a motorcycle accident, her own wrist had ached. It had been difficult to change his bandages or look at the scar where his bone had snapped and torn through flesh without waves folding in her stomach. When they were apart, which was infrequent in their six years, she could imagine his body almost as if she were inside it, seeing what he saw, tasting foods, feeling the bend of his knees, the impact of his feet when he walked.

Now, though, she felt as if his body moved uncomfortably, squeezing in on itself. All she felt was his sadness, and his anger. *How did it happen?* he asked again and again. *Tell me once more,* he'd say, as if the words ever made sense. So she'd tell him: *I went outside. I heard a noise. I looked up. He was on the roof. He stepped off.* Thomas would concentrate, eyebrows tightened, but she could tell that he wasn't hearing her. He didn't want to know. He was unable to hear the story because the story always killed his son.

There had been days she'd stayed in bed on the edge of sleep, resisting wakefulness, yet aware that she was still alive and that she would eventually have to get up, walk, eat, open doors. Sleep was the only tolerable place and even then, dreams invaded, full of lies and false hope. Thomas roamed the house. He stood in the yard. One morning she found him asleep in the car, legs drawn up to his chest on the backseat. He often sat on T's bed, staring at the window—the window from which T had gained access to the roof. T had watched his father make the easy climb from ledge, to dormer, to peak, during chimney cleaning. And Thomas had promised to take T up there for a night of stargazing. She wondered if Thomas blamed himself. But T didn't just fall off the roof. He flew.

"How about there?" Thomas said. She glanced over her shoulder and followed the line of his paddle. He pointed toward the bank and thick woods.

"Sure," she said and the canoe turned. She helped, sweeping her paddle out in a large arc, aiming the bow toward shore. Just before they came aground, she stowed her paddle and jumped out, holding the canoe back before it drove into land. The water wasn't very cold. It soaked the hem of her shorts as she waded, tugging the boat forward. The bottom was mucky and soft, then rocky, and she had to step carefully as she maneuvered the canoe toward a flat place. Thomas waited to get out until the canoe was beached, then he stood and climbed forward over the thwarts, packs, and duffels, and into the water with her.

His skin had darkened, increasing his foreign look. He didn't know much about his history—adopted as a baby. Part Vietnamese. His eyes were wider, more oval toward the bridge of his nose, but his ethnicity, so easily identifiable to others, had become harder for Kate to pinpoint over the years. Yet she loved how Thomas and T's dark hair and olive skin contrasted with hers.

Thomas grabbed hold of the bow deck and yanked, his long ponytail swinging, calves indenting as his muscles hardened. His big toes dug in and left V-shaped marks in the mud. After he hiked up the bank with their paddles, she stepped into his prints and watched as her feet sank into the cool silt. When she looked back at the river, it was as if she were the one moving, not the water. It threw her off balance and she had to touch the canoe and concentrate on the ground to still herself.

Once they'd unloaded the supplies and the canoe was resting on a gunwale in a clearing under tall pines, Kate set up the Coleman stove and sorted through the food. She lined up macaroni and cheese and packages of soup and stew on a rock. The paper was damp and soft. Thomas pulled the cork from the leather cask and filled two metal cups. The wine had a metallic taste; it reminded her of the odor of the canoe. She drank fast. Thomas put some water on to boil, deciding on instant soup, and knelt to regulate the blue flame. With his face down, his cheek bones were rounder—smooth rises that sloped away toward his chin. It was their son's face too, especially when she'd held T in her lap, his head fitting under her chin as she told him bedtime stories.

Once upon a time, she'd told T, there was a boy with dark hair and pretty brown eyes, *just like you,* who found a strange and wonderful umbrella leaning against a tree deep in the forest. On closer inspection, the boy saw that the umbrella was made of shiny black feathers all pulled together and held tight by a grass tie. The sun came through the leaves and made shadows dance on the ground. The boy worked his finger under the reed until it broke, and the whole thing burst open into a dome of ruffling feathers. The handle of the umbrella turned into the head of a bird with a beak and long neck that twisted near his hand, and he took hold.

Thomas had often stood just outside the room, waiting before coming in to kiss T good night. She'd look up and see him in the doorway, serene and thoughtful as he listened. Now she envisioned Thomas peering into that room and seeing only T's empty bed. It made her throat swell. She wished Thomas would glance up at her right now. If he did—if she could just catch his eyes right now—she might be able to say something or *do* something, though she wasn't sure what. He watched the flame, then rose and moved to the packs, rummaging for their mess kits.

The woods had grown dim around them. It might be miles over the hills to any road or town. Or maybe, just beyond the forest, there was a house. There were pines behind their house, and she'd raked paths between them. Then she and T had gathered branches and sticks, leaning them against a tree to make a teepee. They filled in the spaces with leaves and pine needles, or *pineydills,* as T called them. One night Thomas and T slept out there. From the bedroom window she'd sat in the dark and watched their flashlights flicker like giant fireflies going on and off in the woods. It made her happy to think of her two men snuggled together—father and son. Then, that night she'd dreamed that some other man was making love to her. He touched her lightly, running his fingertips over her ribs as if counting them. When she realized that it was not Thomas—not his smell—not his hair sweeping her breasts—she'd jerked awake. Only a dream. Still, she'd gone to the window to assure herself that Thomas was near, but all was dark and for a moment there might not have been a husband or a son out there in the woods.

She hadn't gone to the teepee in the six months since T died. It was probably still there, though the branches had most likely settled and separated or fallen over. There might still be some of T's toy trucks or plastic men underneath. God, she'd have to go dig around for them when they got back. Or maybe not. Let them sink into the earth. Let someone else shovel them up a hundred years from now.

Sometimes she heard T's voice as if he were speaking loudly next to her ear. *Mommy, are dreams real?* She'd flinch and shiver. Once she walked into the living room willing him to be there. For a second she shut her eyes and saw him playing on the rug, his toys surrounding him. Maybe she was in a dream. A nightmare. *Why don't airplanes flap their wings?*

Thomas crouched next to the stove and adjusted the flame. The light went out for an instant, putting him in shadow, and in that moment before the flame burst open again, she felt a surge of panic. The darkness was so eager to swallow everything. She searched for the flashlight in her knapsack, found it, and clicked it on.

"What's the river like tomorrow?" she asked, pulling out the guidebook she'd packed.

"Some falls and unmarked dams to keep an eye out for," Thomas said.

She opened the warped pages and held the light on it. The book described the terrain, the paper mills in Bangor, the falls. Tomorrow they'd pass the Indian reservation in Old Town—an island separated by two branches of the river. Old Town was known for its canoes, and years ago, Thomas had almost bought one at the Old Town Canoe Factory. There was a section on the Penobscot Indians and their legends.

"Gluskap, or Klose-kur-beh, which means 'The Man From Nothing,'" she told Thomas, "was the man who came out of the void—the culture hero—a giant who created all the animals and men. However . . ." She began to read aloud. "'Gluskap was not always successful in his creations. The beaver was made altogether too large and dammed up all the rivers, flooding the valley and placing other creatures in danger of drowning. Gluskap went to visit the beaver and while he spoke, he patted the animal until he got smaller and smaller and became the size he is today.'" She scanned the pages, reading silently. "Here it says that the moose was too large also, but agreed to be nice to man so Gluskap let him stay that size."

Thomas ripped open a package and poured the soup into the boiling water. "No Indian climbed Mount Katahdin until 1804," she said, running her finger down the page. "They were so fearful of it. They believed it was inhabited by evil spirits. One spirit was a huge bird with purple feathers and a woman's face. It would fly down and pick up moose and bear. 'Once,'" she read, "'a small boy was picking blueberries when a giant bird soared from the cliffs, plucked him up with her talons and flew away.'" She glanced up. Thomas put a hand over his eyes. She closed the guide. His shoulders shook.

"I'm sorry," she said and started to get up, to go to him, but he held out his hand for her to stop.

When she was little, Kate and her brother would snuggle next to their father, listening to stories. They helped to make them up. Some stories never ended. They went on for weeks and weeks until they evolved into other stories. She'd wanted to fly too. Dreamed of flying—that wonderful sensation of lifting off the ground. Climbed a tree and felt the wind lift her hair. Imagined, but only imagined. She'd seen T, his small face full of wonder, intent on anything that flew: milkweed, bed sheets on the line, newspaper caught in the wind. Birds.

The magic umbrella carried the boy over rooftops and fields, his shadow running across the earth below.

Kate felt T's body pressed against her chest—the softness of his skin, his sweet sun smell—as if he were in her arms for just that instant of remembering. Then he was gone.

Thomas lay beside her. She heard him breathing, then wiggling, adjusting his body to the hard ground. She shut her eyes and felt the river; even zipped into her sleeping bag, the motion stayed with her. The landscape passed by, brown, gray, green. Sky and land and water. Whirls and circles of light. She saw rills and wrinkles pillowing above some concealed object and started, opened her eyes. There was a space above their site—a little break between the trees, revealing the sky and stars. She gazed into it until the opening seemed to close up, grow blacker. Maybe the tree branches had caught the wind and changed shape, but there was hardly any breeze. It had been more like a blotting out of the stars—an object, passing overhead. An owl, perhaps.

"Did you see that?" she whispered.

"What?" Thomas mumbled. He lay on his side.

Then it came again. Was it her own eyelids creeping down like curtains? She let go as if lying on her back submerged in water, sounds muffled. She sank to the bottom of the river and watched a shadow slide over the surface and away.

I went outside. I heard a noise. I looked up. At first she'd thought it was a giant black bird perched on the peak of the house. She shielded her eyes against the sun to see the silhouette of her boy. He held an umbrella above his head. There was a moment of balance when he had one foot on and one off. Then everything pulled up—his clothes, his hair, his mouth—and he fell. His umbrella tumbled away. She gasped. Her body went forward as if to hurl itself under him.

Kate flung her sleeping bag back and got her arms out.

"Hush," Thomas said. "You're dreaming." He reached behind himself and patted her. It was as though she'd been stopped suddenly, wrenched backwards. He left his hand on her stomach as if to hold her in place. She concentrated on the weight of his hand, absorbing that small warm pressure. It had been so long since he'd touched her. Then he removed his hand. She smelled propane and dirt and his familiar sweat, like the rich humid heat inside a greenhouse. She rolled on her side, moved closer, pressed her mouth against the skin on the back of his neck. He shifted and curled away. She held her breath, drew her lips together, tasted salt.

When she woke, Thomas was standing over the Coleman stove and the coffee pot perked. The river beyond was gray, like the overcast sky.

"Is it going to rain?" she asked.

"You better get up," he said and knelt, turned the gas off.

They drank coffee in silence, packed, then launched. The sun was trying to break through the haze. If it did, she'd have to rub on more lotion and put her shirt over her bathing suit. The surface of the water was smooth, reflecting the hills and now her head as she leaned out. Her image traveled along next to the canoe—a rippling shadow face, no features. It was as if there were some other being down there gazing up at her. A ghost person who lived inside the reflection. Perhaps a hand would emerge, dripping and gentle. A finger might touch her skin.

"Are you going to help?" Thomas said. She'd stopped paddling. His paddle went under and came up, drizzling water as he used a J-stroke to make up the difference. His strokes extended into the perimeters of her vision. "Kate," he said.

There was an edge of anger in his tone. Then in a near whisper he said, "We should get some distance behind us."

She sat straight and lifted her paddle. She imagined that Thomas watched her back, her shoulder blades working in a circle with the rhythm of her stroke. She felt him matching her beat, drawing his paddle through the water, maybe with some restraint, in order to keep the canoe even. She dug in, staring at the farthest point ahead where the river and trees seemed to come together like a wall, though she knew it was just the mirage of distance. *Distance* was dark forest green, nearly black. It was another time, long ago when they were young. Once upon a time on another river. When they swam naked under a moonlit sky. And made love, half floating in the shallows.

That afternoon they passed through several small towns, and then corn fields. Some cows stood up to their knees in the water and raised their heads as the canoe approached and glided by. *Moocows*.

A while later, the river forked and they took the east branch. Soon a steel bridge came into view, crossing over the river. People stood in the center of it, leaning on the green girders. As the canoe drifted closer, Kate saw that they were teenage boys.

"The reservation," Thomas said.

The boys smoked cigarettes and hung over the railing, their straight black hair long and shining as they peered down. Cigarettes fell in the water on either side of the canoe. Underneath the bridge it was cool and quiet. When the canoe slid out the other side, the boys had crossed over.

"Tourists!" a boy yelled. He brought his hands together as if he held a camera and pretended to take a picture. A cigarette landed in the bottom of the canoe just behind Kate's feet and hissed in the moisture there.

"Ignore them," Thomas said.

"Hey, lady," one of the boys yelled. She looked over her shoulder to see a lanky boy standing on an upper joist. He balanced on the beam, his arms out. He tottered.

Kate let go of her paddle and it clattered to the floor of the canoe. She stood, turning. The canoe wobbled and Thomas yelled for her to sit down. Her shins bumped the metal seat, throwing her sideways. The canoe rocked, and water gushed over the gunwale and sloshed to the other side and back. Thomas slammed his paddle to the bottom of the canoe and grabbed her by the wrist. The boys hooted and yelled. The boy on the beam waved. Thomas's fingers dug into her skin.

"Jesus Christ," he said. "We almost capsized."

Kate's legs trembled and her side hurt where she'd pitched and banged against the gunwale. Water in the bottom of the canoe eddied and lapped against their duffels. She looked at Thomas's hand, still clenching her arm. She crouched, then he let go, climbed back, and slid his paddle out from under the thwarts. They'd drifted twenty yards or so past the bridge.

Over Thomas's shoulder, on a rise near the end of the bridge, she saw a white teepee-like structure, red stripes circling its peak. A sign near the top read Indian Moccasins, and an American flag hung from a pole below.

"We need to bail," Thomas said.

Thomas turned the canoe toward shore and edged it against the bank so they wouldn't drift. They used sponges to soak up the water and squeeze it overboard.

"Hey, mister," one of the boys called from the bridge. "Are you Indian?"

Thomas lifted his chin slightly, smiled. "No," he said. "Part Vietnamese."

The boy nodded thoughtfully, then said, "It's hard to tell sometimes."

Thomas glanced at Kate. It was an instant of recognition, or remembering—all the questions they'd endured—but then Thomas frowned, slid his eyes away from her, and it felt as if her lungs had filled too much, too fast.

Occasionally, when she'd been with T, people stared. T's dark hair and Asian eyes in contrast to her lightness made them curious. Adopted—is what their looks said, unless Thomas was with her, and then they realized T *was* her child. Once in a restaurant in Northlee a man had spoken to her as she passed his table on the way back from the restroom. "Gook lover," he said. At first she couldn't believe she'd heard correctly, but when she turned toward him, to be sure, she saw the hatred in his face. A chill crept over her. The man took a sip of his coffee, smacked his lips. He hunched forward, gray eyes glaring at her. She'd looked away. Evil. That was the only way to describe it to Thomas later. Thomas had nodded, then put his hand on top of T's head, smoothing his hair.

When the canoe was dry, Thomas shoved them away from shore. The air had the faint smell of rotten eggs and smoke. Kate turned to see that the boys on the bridge had lost interest in them and were talking and puffing on their cigarettes.

"I wonder if that's all they do all day," Kate said.

"When I was here before," Thomas said, "looking to buy that canoe, I remember the sales clerk telling me that the Indian boys weren't allowed to cross the bridge into Old Town. They weren't welcome over there because they always got into trouble."

"Sad," she said. "Amazing too, considering there used to be over forty thousand Indians in Maine alone. I read there are only four hundred or so here." She looked toward the island shore. Just an island—floating, set apart. Deals with the government—a reservation. A haven. Not so safe.

"Poor kids," Thomas said. "A culture disappearing."

Kate turned her ear toward him. "You think?" she said.

"Who will be left to tell them? Who will remember anything?"

"There are those tales," she said. "Gluskap, their creator. That's a beautiful story." She looked over her shoulder. Thomas stared into the water, following the sweep of his paddle.

"When I was a kid," he said, "I used to make things up about my past. I didn't even look like my parents. It was as if I didn't come from anywhere."

She'd heard Thomas speak of this before, but now she thought she understood more clearly. Looking into T's face must have been like seeing the link to his heritage. Losing T was like losing his past. And his future.

"Hey!" a boy yelled from the bridge. Kate looked back. The boy—maybe ten or eleven years old—used his cigarette to point toward the water below. "Route 1 is a lot quicker."

She turned and paddled. T would never smoke cigarettes or take drugs. He'd never drown or get killed in a car wreck. He'd never feel the stares of racism. He'd never even reach the age of those boys on the bridge. She would have protected T from those things. If she could. Maybe T was safe.

Then it came to her again. The mountain where she'd grown up—that fresh, new green spreading down the hill into the valley, and realizing that her father wasn't there to see it or smell it ever again. She was just a girl and it was so hard to imagine that he would no longer stand with her on the front porch, taking a deep breath and saying the things he always said: *The mountain is waking up! Stretching her feet.* It seemed as if the loss of her father had stayed inside her all her life, like an ache pushing up through everything else—until T's death, and then those memories had dissolved, or become less. Obscured, covered over.

She and Thomas hadn't planned T, but then he was there and so their lives had changed, and they'd married and loved their son more than they ever thought possible. More than each other, perhaps, because now they were spinning apart. Without Thomas, who would she be? The past would evaporate. It would be like being dead. And then, she thought, not existing might be a relief.

After an hour or so, the smell that had edged its way in little by little came upon them full force. A foul, sulfur odor. Around the bend they found themselves behind a paper mill. The surface was nearly solid with floating logs. An orange-yellow foam caught between the logs and gathered in bubbly islands. The canoe pierced the stuff and carried it along as they cut between, bumping the barkless trunks and rolling them apart. The stench was bad, fetid—punky wood soaked in sour milk. Kate retched and stabbed at the spaces between the logs, trying to find a faster way through.

There were people living here—ranches and trailers lined the bank on the other side, the paint flaking off from years of dank smoke. Some children waved to them and ran under clotheslines down to the water's edge. She squinted, her eyes burning. One child—a little girl—swung her arm above her head, her hips going back and forth in her enthusiasm.

Kate started to raise her paddle as a greeting, but there was no time. She needed air.

Once they'd traveled far enough downstream to breathe easily again, Thomas said, "They must get used to it." The logs stayed behind, corralled by a series of gates they'd had to maneuver through, but one yellow log up ahead lolled on the surface like an overturned boat.

"Dead ahead," she said.

"I see it," he said, and they passed to the left of it.

A wind came up, blowing her hair back and putting resistance against the canoe. She jabbed her paddle in and down and back, feathering it forward. Her arm muscles strained, and she leaned into it, putting her body behind each stroke. Her skin felt prickly. The water, still deep, was becoming turbulent. She glanced over her shoulder. Thomas looked past her as if to indicate that she should keep an eye out. The water was fast. She turned away and paddled hard. She could imagine that she was alone. The canoe might have broken in half, and she'd surged on without him. There was a break in the surface—a line cutting all the way across the river. Suddenly the canoe turned and was dragged sideways.

"Pull to, pull to!" Thomas yelled behind her. He was reaching and jamming his paddle into the swirl, trying to get them straight. Now she saw the edge, only a few feet ahead. A drop off. A dam, or falls, unmarked, water rushing over it, dragging them. She back-paddled, pushing the water. The current was too strong. They had no power; they were being sucked over. The canoe spun so Thomas's end was downstream and she was upstream. They tried paddling forward, but it was too late. She caught sight of the curved transparent horizon where the water bent and fell. There might have been a second when the canoe hung over the edge—Thomas's end out in space.

She felt the impact, the jar of the stern striking rock, but then she was in the air. Something fell with her, just before her—a duffel—and she was shoved under. Her temples felt pressed. There was a numbing cold and pain in her shoulders. Pebbles and sand scraped her knees. She tried to rise, but her hands couldn't find anything to push off of, to give her leverage. The pounding water kept her down. She couldn't breathe. When she gave up, the current carried her out, and she was lifted, almost gently, into calm water. Her feet skimmed the bottom. She stood. The water came to her knees. She bent down, touched the surface, trying to get her balance.

"Thomas!" she yelled. She twisted, searching. She saw the drop-off where water poured over a broken structure of cement and rock—about a five-foot drop. She put her hand on her forehead. Her fingers felt large and icy. Water circled her legs and the light seemed overwhelmingly bright. For a moment she considered shutting her eyes, dropping down, sinking beneath the surface. Suddenly the canoe popped out of the swirl and shot toward shore. It caught in a web of branches. The bow nudged the bank as if the canoe were alive, trying to find its own way out.

"Thomas!" she yelled again. There was a roar in her ears, the dam, the rushing water. He was nowhere. He was gone. She splashed through the water, dragging her hands below the surface, feeling. Her feet were numb.

"Here," Thomas said. He stood only a few feet behind her in the turbulence. Blood ran from his eye. He reached to touch his own cheek, wobbled, and fell over.

The water was thick around her legs as she ran toward him. She reached down, grabbed his head and pulled his face into the air. The blood had washed away, but now started to trickle again from a gash on his forehead. She got her hands under his arms and dragged him. His skin felt rubbery. The shore was mostly gravel, but there was a stretch of sand. He was heavier out of the water, and she worried for the skin on his back and legs as she inched him onto land. He groaned, came conscious. She knelt next to him and put her palm over his wound.

"I'm okay," he said, his eyes shut.

"Open your eyes," she said. He obeyed and she saw that his pupils were tiny. Then they dilated; he focused on her.

"The canoe?" he said.

"Don't worry," she said. "It's there." She could see it, trapped, rocking. "You have a cut," she said.

"Feels okay," he said and reached to touch his head, but then his hand dropped. "Going to be sick," he said.

She helped him turn on his side, keeping her hand on his forehead while he vomited, mostly water. She held his ponytail away, curled it around her fist, wringing it out. Drops fell on his back. When he lay down again, blood ran between her fingers. The gash wasn't very large, though. She took off her wet shirt, balled it up, and held it to his head.

"Can you hold this?" she asked, and he put his hand on it. He had goose bumps, but the sun beat down and the sand was warm. She brushed some grit off his cheek, then went after the canoe.

When she brought the canoe up, Thomas's eyes were closed, but he still held the shirt to his head. She waded back into the water to search for their gear. Almost immediately her feet met with a duffel. She reached down and put her hand around the strap. It was water-logged and hard to lift, but she got it out in jerks. When she found their sleeping bags, she laid them out in the sun to dry. She located the first aid kit in one of their packs; the cloth bandages were in plastic bags and dry. There was antibiotic ointment.

"Let me look," she said to Thomas. He dropped her shirt away from his head. The bleeding had slowed. She dabbed the cut with the shirt and fingered ointment over the area, then covered it with a thick square of cheesecloth and wrapped longer pieces around his head. Thomas let her do all this, his eyes shut, not saying anything.

"I think you should talk to me a little," she said. "I'm worried about concussion."

"Aspirin?" he said. She got him some, found a cup and filled it from the water jug she'd dragged out. "I think I'm okay," he said. "Just let me lie here for a while."

The Coleman stove was ruined. The food box was gone and she finally gave up, came ashore and lay down next to Thomas. The sun was warm on her back, which made her feel better. She lay her cheek against the sand. She watched Thomas's chest rising and falling as he breathed. Above him, the trees towered—ash and poplar—their leaves verdant. The bandage looked all right. She touched her own forehead. Her skin felt smooth, tight from the sun and cold water. It didn't hurt.

She was exhausted. Her limbs felt stretched. She shut her eyes. Tears—she hadn't known they were there—dripped, pushed out in a blink. It seemed strange that her body could give them up without her being aware. There had been so many tears—her mother couldn't stop crying at T's funeral. She'd lost her husband so young, now her grandson—a little boy, she'd always said, who had his grandfather's laugh. Kate couldn't imagine when the ache would ever end, probably never. She tried to remember what their lives were like before this pain. There was Thomas across a room at a friend's party. People walked between them, or stood in groups, shifting so he came in and out of view. She barely knew his name, but her eyes couldn't stop finding him. His chin, his dark hair, his fingers, holding a glass. Later he would say, *I knew exactly where you were at every moment.* And later, when T was a baby, they took him to her mother's place on the mountain. That night Thomas had stood on the front porch and held T out, his small legs dangling, as if presenting their son to the dark horizon, the stars glittering above the summit. T had laughed, and Thomas had swept him down, then up. Into the air again.

It felt that all these things happened before they happened, and now again after they happened. It was as if everything existed all at once, going forward or backwards, into the past or future. Or standing still. For a moment, she saw through to the place where the pain blurred—a blue fog—as if she could drift into it, diffuse it with a breath.

It was a cool night. The mosquitoes weren't too bad, still she set up the tarps, making a tent with the canoe. The sleeping bags had dried nicely. She spread them out and helped Thomas crawl underneath. She pulled the screening around and lay back next to him, their heads under the canoe. They were on land. They were okay. She stared into the dark.

"Kate," Thomas said. He sounded delirious, talking in his sleep.

"I'm here," she said.

"T?" he said.

She swallowed. "He's safe," she whispered.

Thomas sighed. "For a second," he said. "I forgot. Started to dream."

"I understand," she said and put her hand on his shoulder. "You feel better?"

"Aspirin kicked in," he said.

"I'm sorry," she said. "I didn't see it until it was too late."

"I know," he said.

Too late. Maybe if he'd held tight, the umbrella would have slowed his fall. He hit the ground. A muffled clap. There was that sound. When she got to him, he wasn't moving. He was still. The ground stopped him. His legs and arms were splayed. She'd knelt down, touched his neck. Then she was running and not running. She was next to her child, keeping him in her vision, but also leaving him and running to the phone. And then she was standing above the EMTs, who lifted T's body, and shook their heads, and said words she couldn't hear. Then she was still kneeling over T's body, or running again.

Kate shut her eyes and saw the river, felt it pulling her along. She went with it, reminding herself that she was on land, no unmarked dams to watch for. Nothing to fall off of. Water. Air on her face. T had fallen through the air. Into air. *Air* was white, then clear. Invisible.

She felt breath on her cheek. Then lips grazed her earlobe. Fingers slid down her neck, stopped on her collar bone, then moved again, found her breast. She breathed, shifted slightly. Felt as if she was filling with something. Joy. *Joy* was blue and red at the edges. It was her heart pumping. His hand smoothed over her ribs and reached around her. She thought to touch his head, to make sure the bandages were in place, but her arms were too heavy. She couldn't lift them. He moved on top of her, spread her legs apart with his own. She was sinking; the river motion was too fast, dragging her under. She saw the drop-off. Smelled sour milk. How could she let her body fill up with joy? Hands lifted her hips. She twisted, jerked, and came awake.

Thomas lay next to her; the even breathing of his sleep echoed under the canoe. It sounded like pine branches sweeping the aluminum. No one was touching her.

Neither of them spoke as they righted the canoe and carried it down to the water. When they woke, Thomas had said he felt okay, just a little woozy. He was hungry, anxious to get to the bay. Kate swung their gear into the canoe with a bang, no organization. She climbed in and went forward to her spot, waited. Thomas shoved them free.

The river was narrow, a little fast, and she was jittery as the canoe slid along, finding its way through swirls and spins. She felt as though her knees had become a part of the canoe. Her hips the gunwales. It was as if the canoe had absorbed her and she'd fallen into its dream of land and sky and water—into some other world where time didn't exist, and inside it, she was free.

Then the river grew wide and deep. After a while a waterline appeared along the rocky shore.

"Salt," Thomas said. She turned to see him lick his fingers. He dipped his hand in again and tasted once more. "We're close."

She held her paddle with one hand, reached down and pressed her other hand underneath the surface. Soon they would come out at the bay. The ocean would loom in front of them. If only they could keep going—never stop. Head for the horizon—the edge of the earth.

"Come on now," Thomas said. "We're almost done."

She drew her knees up and turned, swung her legs around so she was on her seat, facing him. He sighed and laid his paddle across the gunwale. The cloth bandage drooped above his eye.

"Okay," he said. "We'll just drift wherever." They faced each other, holding their paddles. "I need to get out," he said.

At first she thought he meant that he had to get out of the canoe. "You mean leave," she said. "Leave the house?" Leave me? She couldn't say it out loud.

"I don't know what I mean," he said.

"I hate that house," she said. Her eyes burned. She meant she hated the roof and the goddamn peak of the roof. The shaft of her paddle bumped against the gunwale and flipped out of her hands into the water.

Thomas picked up his paddle and stabbed at the water, but her paddle floated out of reach. "Jesus," he said.

"He believed he could fly," she said.

Thomas stopped paddling. He leaned back slightly. "Why?" he said. And then he laid his paddle down. "Why? For God's sake. Other children do not jump off roofs. They do not *believe* they can fly."

"He was different," she said.

Thomas shook his head. Tears fell from his eyes. "I can't stand it," he said. "I can't stand it another minute. It's too much. Every day. Too much."

"I know," she said softly.

He sucked tears off his lips and into his mouth. Then he looked at her, his head tipped slightly.

"You do," he said, not as a question, but in confirmation, as if realizing that she did know—that she was the one other person in the world who really did know. He scooped a handful of water and splashed his face. "I told him I'd take him up there sometime. He watched me climb out there."

She swallowed, but her mouth was dry and it made her cough.

"It was my fault," she said. "It was that horrid, evil story."

Thomas shook his head. "No," he said. "You can't say that. It's a part of who he is. Who he was." He began to sob. "I don't want to think of him falling anymore. He didn't. He flew."

Her eyes ached—blues and greens and light bouncing off the water. She gazed at Thomas, seeing T in his face. Seeing herself. Thomas's face was her face. There were other stories, but this was the one they had made together and would keep. Would remember together. The beautiful boy who believed he could fly. And did.

She moved forward, caught him in her arms, their knees pressing into each other and against wet duffels. He gripped her shoulders and put his face against her chest. She looked over his head toward the stern. Her paddle drifted farther away, breaking the reflection on the surface, and a breeze, full of the smell of sea air, skirted across the water. Sunlight glinted off tiny swells and the canoe rocked gently. She felt her husband's heart beating, his moist skin, their bones fitting together. Lush hills rose up on either side as if they were floating in the crease of a giant palm.

The Matter of Dawn

THAT COMETS ARE SAID TO PORTEND DISASTER, famine, and other unfavorable events is not foremost in the minds of David and Anna who stand together, arm in arm, eyes skyward. To them, a glimpse of this rare phenomenon is fortuitous—a natural wonder that also happens to coincide with their reunion after nine years.

The comet is wonderful to see—its hazy tail of dust and gas trailing behind is much like a child's drawing. A black crayon sky over bright yellow paper, squiggles scratched out with a fingernail. The comet appears stilled in the heavens, yet it is driving forward at 176,000 kilometers an hour.

"So beautiful," says Anna. She has recently traveled from Colorado to meet with David after all these years. He has been courting her via e-mail for some months now.

"You know what it means," says David. "Us, forever and ever." He pulls her close and they stare at the sky. They are slightly drunk from sitting in the bar for five hours, eating nachos, drinking beers, and holding hands. Perhaps, if all goes well, the comet's appearance will be a happy detail in the recounting of this date as told to their future offspring.

There is evidence, however, already to the contrary, as there always is. First of all, Hale-Bopp's memory is forever tainted by those poor deluded souls whose suicides recently covered the front page of every newspaper. Though the romantic-minded would like to pose that perhaps those men and women of the cult Heaven's Gate are safely aboard a spaceship now, transformed into children, and ready with the odd things they packed—quarters and lip balm—the pragmatist knows a fatal fantasy has been played out. Jokes have already circled the planet, flown through the Internet in a matter of seconds. Quarters for cosmic tolls.

Secondly, there is the matter of David's past. He hasn't been completely honest with Anna, or himself, about a previous relationship—one he hasn't quite ended yet, and so *previous* isn't the right word at all. *Ongoing* would be more accurate.

Disaster is always a possibility.

But wait. There is the celestial body overhead and here are David and Anna, full of hope and good intentions, standing just outside the restaurant by the Atlantic ocean on this unusually warm March evening.

A few minutes later, before David drops Anna off at a friend's house where she's staying, they'll make their own private joke. They'll say that they should name their firstborn Hale-Bopp. Or at least Haley, if it's a girl, though then the history of her name might be confused with a different comet: Halley's comet. No matter. A boy could be Hale. Anna can imagine David holding an infant, kissing its tiny fingertips one by one and saying, "Hello little Hale-Bopp. My little bop."

Their first meeting at the restaurant was on neutral ground, but now it's two days later and Anna has left the coast and headed inland to visit David on his own turf for the first time. After a spirited greeting from David's dog, a prancing, tail-wagging, three-year-old German shepherd named Traven, Anna stands in David's living room. David says he's nervous about how closely she is looking at everything. What does she make of it? This, his home, and his life here in the New Hampshire woods, not far from the mountain where he grew up. She smiles at him, nods so he will understand that she's not ready to say. She needs to walk from room to room slowly. There is a lot to see. Much to take in. A gargoyle face, pinned to the stones above the fireplace. A jar of red tulips, sagging with heavy heads on the sunny wooden table. "For you," David says. An aluminum tray on a windowsill—ten dirt-filled cups, sprouting green-white shoots, bent toward the light. Tomatoes. Black bronze figures on shelves and sills—delicate, pinched metal: an Asian man carrying a bundle on his shoulder; a woman on her knees, her torso headless and half-armed; a wiry tree, the branches tangled and coming to buds at the ends, like Medusa's hair.

"My parents," David says, when she stops in front of a framed black-and-white photograph of a couple on their wedding day. The train of the bride's gown spreads in a lacy, ice-white pool at the feet of the newlyweds. Anna looks for David in his father's face. The resemblance is there—dark eyebrows over serious eyes. The chin is strongly dimpled. David wears a beard. His mother is beautiful—long blond braid, a gentle, welcoming smile. Anna knows that David's father died when he was a boy. His mother, now in her sixties, still spends summers in a cabin she and her husband built together when they were young. She never remarried; it's a sad but romantic story.

A tall basket by the fireplace holds an array of wooden canes, each with a handle carved into the shape of an animal head—a bird, an elephant, a weasel. The room is filled with so many odd things—accumulations from travel, from a forty-year life. Objects that reveal much more about David's tastes than she'd gleaned through e-mail. She isn't displeased. Each ornament is like a word, or a whole phrase—much more flowery than his usual, spare sentences. And everything has its careful place—much tidier than the typos in his e-mails. His program, he once apologized, won't let him scroll back or delete.

On one dark wall, a painting of a nude. The woman is standing, curving to the side, arms above her head. Long reddish-brown hair.

David puts his hands on Anna's shoulders as she gazes at the painting.

"She's like you," he says.

"You've never seen me," she teases. She means naked.

"The hair," he says. "It's what I always remembered about you. Your beautiful burgundy hair." He puts his nose in her hair, in her neck, and she tips her head to the side, to let him.

There is the bedroom and she stands in the doorway, doesn't quite dare go all the way in. There is the bed. Dark wood headboard and tall rounded posts at the foot. White comforter. White walls. The room is sparse, no pictures on the walls. A bureau and a braided rug. And the bed. Sunlight falls in rhomboid checkers over the bedding. A many-paned window above the bed. It's winter but the window is open a few inches. Water drips off the eaves outside and it sounds like rain. She feels the cool air through the window and when she steps back, away from the room, he is right behind her. He turns her to face him, and kisses her hard.

There are books. Hundreds of books in the office and the computer where he writes the messages. For a moment she imagines him sitting in the blue swivel chair, fingers on the keyboard, staring at the screen, typing words for her. The words that brought her back. Brought her here after so many years. He was her teacher, and married then, so they never spoke of their attraction, until they found each other through e-mail and began a correspondence that has led to this reunion, this quixotic (they're not unaware of the potential for artfulness in missives, electronic or otherwise) quest for true love.

Anna can't help but feel that she has moved faster than e-mail, catching a plane and arriving on the East Coast in four and a half hours. In those hours she has become flesh and blood, standing in front of David, making all the words—his full, sumptuous, slippery, sweet words—take responsibility for themselves.

There is the guest room. Toys. Piles of children's toys. Plastic things, red and blue and green. A yellow truck with big black wheels. Plastic, stiff little men, with stiff-raised arms, lined on the windowsill. The room for guests—where she'll stay, they've joked—but she knows they'll sleep together. It's been inevitable since the first kiss as Hale-Bopp crossed the heavens two nights ago on their first date. Though there are rules—lines to draw—because of the other woman. The woman who is the mother of the child. Not David's child, hers alone. The woman who has been David's on-again, off-again lover.

Sometjing I have to tell u you. A casual thing. No committtments. She doesn't live here, but sometimes stays. write back quick. Tell me you junderstand.

The woman, whose name is Dawn, is out of town for the night.

Though Anna was not unaware of Dawn, it isn't until she sees the child's toys in the guest room that she realizes the true presence of the woman.

She wants to leave now. She wishes she'd never come. Her legs feel weak and she could cry. His hand is on the doorknob, still holding the door wide to the guest room, and she is standing just in front of him, inside the crook of his arm and his chest, as if caught there. She can't go forward or step back. He keeps the door open as if he means for her to take a good look. He doesn't want any secrets. Though she can't help but think that she is the secret—the secret visitor. She knows he hasn't told Dawn about her—the invisible e-woman. Anna stares into the room, though she wants to shut her eyes. This is the guest room where the child sleeps when he comes here. Comes here with his mother who lies on the white bed with David. The mother who stretches with her arms above her head. Her hips, the curve of her waist. Anna doesn't know what color Dawn's hair is. Dawn lies on the bed and David lies next to her, on top of her, and in the other room is the child.

In Boulder, Anna has had no lover in a long time. No man spoons her body into his. *I'm a born again virgin*, she wrote to David when they first made contact and began telling each other what they'd been up to in the last nine years. The medium, safe behind a keyboard, made it easy to speak freely, to write openly.

Never married? Kids? David asked. *What's the deal?*

I guess I never met anyone I wanted to marry, she answered, trying to remember if there was any man who might have ever asked her.

E-mail may be immediate, but it is also blind and selective. She could choose which questions to answer, and which not. For instance, the one about kids: somewhere in the universe is a girl, not hers anymore, not since she gave birth at seventeen, but hers all the same. A daughter, given up for adoption.

Anna knows only two possible things about her daughter: she is eighteen years old, or she's dead. Neither piece of information helps to quell the sometimes desperate sadness Anna feels when she remembers her—a child she didn't love, no, couldn't love, but does love. And so love spills out into nowhere, to no one, for no reason.

The fact is, Anna's daughter, whose name is Alice, is at this very moment ecstatic because a boy she's had a crush on for some months now has just asked her out. That Alice and her parents live in New Hampshire, a mere eighty-eight miles from where David and Anna stand now, doesn't matter. Anna will never meet Alice; she'll never know if her daughter is living or dead. For Anna, Alice will always be as ethereal and ephemeral as a burst of imagination.

David pulls the guest bedroom door closed and watches as Anna moves on to the next room. She looks smaller, somehow. Where before her arms were crossed in contemplation, now it seems she's freezing. He thinks maybe he should offer her a sweater. He thinks maybe he should have shoved the toys under the bed.

He's a bit unsure of what to do, or say. When she wrote, saying she'd be in his area, visiting an old graduate school friend who happens to live just over the border in Maine, he couldn't not see her. Of course they'd meet. More than anything he wanted to see her. But now he must determine if his feelings for her are something more than quick sentences scrolling down a screen. More even than the kisses and hand-holding they came to so easily.

He must also decide if Dawn and he are indeed finished. But how could he know anything until he met Anna in person? The sexy-worded sensual writer who appears via e-mail twice, sometimes three times a day.

Anna stops in front of the fireplace. Later he'll build a fire and they can lean against one another. That they can do that, touch each other finally, is amazing to him and it reminds him of the past—of the days at school nine years ago when he found himself longing for her to come by his office. How he couldn't stop thinking about her. She'd sit across from him, holding her papers and looking down. He'd wanted to reach out and tuck her hair back behind her ear. He wanted to tell her how beautiful her eyes were—full of texture and light, like dark suede brushed one way, then the other—and once he nearly did, but stopped himself. He was married then. Anna was a student. She was prim and diffident, all neat-skirted and careful responses. He imagines she respects him for never having said anything, and he's glad she knows he was faithful to his wife for their entire marriage. It thrilled him when Anna e-mailed her own confession: *Back then I had a fantasy about making love with you on your desk.*

"Do you want to borrow a sweater?" he asks her now.

She smiles and shakes her head. "No, I'm fine," she says. Her voice is soft and airy-sweet. Shy. So unlike the stories that poured from her fingers to his computer screen. Such a different woman in those words. It's as if she'd let him into her brain and taken him on a tour. But here, in reality, it isn't so easy to get inside her. He can tell that the toys in the guest room bothered her, but he can only guess how much and why.

He wrote her once that he didn't have much interest in kids, though he'd adored his sister Kate's boy, his only nephew, who'd died tragically. After that, he'd tried not to care so much, but Dawn's child opened him up a little. No, a lot. He loves that little boy.

The boy, whose name is Dillon, is at this moment on the other side of town with a babysitter. Dillon is a lovely child. A spirit of innocence. He likes to sing songs to David (*There are bears bears bears everywheres wheres wheres and I don't cares cares cares any more)*, and it's not unlikely that Dillon, who has just gotten off the bus from school, might ask the babysitter (a friend of Dawn's and a student of David's), to visit the man whom he has come to love as a father. The man who is his mother's boyfriend. The funny, roughhouse man who also owns a German shepherd named Traven. Dillon loves Traven too.

Dawn, driving south for her tenth high school reunion, is thinking at this moment that not only did she forget to pack her own toothbrush, but she forgot to put Dillon's into his overnight knapsack. If that's all she's forgotten, everything will be fine. He can go a night without brushing; it won't damage him for life. She cringes; she hates it when she thinks things like that. How many little things add up to damage?

She checks her face in the rearview and thinks of her ex-husband. How many punches did she endure until she'd had enough? Her eyes are blue-green, and more on the blue side in this late afternoon light. After her divorce, she threw out all face makeup. She'd used it to cover bruises mostly. She looks okay, not bad, hair still blond as it ever was in high school. She hasn't changed that much—just the slight tilt of her nose from where he broke it that time.

David can't understand how she could have stayed with the man so long. Sometimes she can't either, but everything is more complicated than that. Lately, she's tired of explaining herself to David. She gets the feeling that he doesn't quite see her for who she is. She's afraid he pities her, thinks he's rescuing her from something, and it makes her uncomfortable. He's great with Dillon. She's happy for that. Though their growing affection worries her too. David's twelve years older than she is; it's a gap they can't always ignore. He couldn't believe it when he figured out she wasn't even born when the astronauts first landed on the moon. Then he got mad when she suggested that maybe the whole walk on the moon thing was a hoax. It could be, why not? A government conspiracy. They've covered up things before. It's not that she really gives credence to this, either; it's David's attitude she pushes against. Keeping an open mind, allowing for other possibilities does not always a nut make. In fact, it's what's given her hope when things were really bad. She and David believe in different things.

She'll buy a toothbrush for herself when she stops for cigarettes, even though she quit smoking two weeks ago when David told her she smelled like an ashtray. Right now she wants a cigarette more than anything; she's a bit nervous about the reunion. She has nothing to say to anyone. No great successes to report. A failed marriage. She can't imagine telling anyone about the college degree she's been hacking away at part time for the last five years. Or the waitress job. She can tell them about Dillon. Her pride and joy. She's going to get that college degree, and then a stable job with good benefits so she can give her son everything he deserves, though she tries to give him everything now. She does pretty well. David helps sometimes too (he's the sweetest man she's ever known), though she'd rather do it herself.

The thing Dawn has neglected (out of financial impossibility) is regular car maintenance. Right now the fan belt is well worn, and fraying rapidly on one edge. It has not yet snapped, though it's under intense pressure and whirring around pulleys at several hundred revolutions per minute.

In her early twenties, Anna had an affair with a married man. They lasted about eight months. She learned that you cannot love a married man because he is always a liar and you can never forget it. She doesn't want a married man and though David isn't married, the toys in the guest room and the way David stiffens and lets the machine answer the phone makes her recall the always-kept-out-of-sight, anonymous role she played as the other woman. She swore she'd never play it again.

There is a worn, pinkish couch in front of the fireplace. The gargoyle stares at her. Open, scallop-lipped mouth, devil's eyes.

"Are you all right?" David asks. He's standing behind her, looking over her shoulder.

"I like this face," she says and touches the ceramic, covers its whole face with her palm.

"I like him too," David says. He slides his arms around her waist, hands on her belly, and pulls her back into him. "Is it awful?" he says.

She reaches an arm up over her shoulder and puts her hand on his cheek. She's not exactly sure what he's referring to. "It's a beautiful house," she says. The water is dripping outside the window, dangling in sparkling chains.

David lets go of her when Traven barks at the door.

It is late afternoon and if they want to hike the small mountain behind David's house, they should do it now before the light fades. It's hard to leave the couch where they've been kissing for the better part of an hour. *Disheveled* is a good word. They stand, shake themselves, and put on coats, scarves, gloves. David has two pairs of snowshoes. It doesn't escape Anna's notice that David is ready with things for two. Two tennis rackets stabbed on a wall peg.

"The only part that worries me," June, Anna's friend, said last night as they sipped margaritas at June's kitchen table, "is the thing he still has going on with that single mother person."

"I know, " Anna said. "But it's not serious."

"Then why hasn't he told her about you?" June asked.

"A good question." She agreed, though she could think of a million excuses for him—one being that they hadn't seen each other in almost ten years. What if she'd turned into a big, fat blob with a face like dog food? Who could blame him for holding off?

"Come on," June said. "I'm sure you're the best wagon to roll through his town ever. He's got to see that."

"I hope so," she said. "It feels right, you know. Like magic." She toasted her glass toward the window. "Like yonder comet."

"I could vomit on that freaking comet," June said. "I've had nothing but bad luck since the thing came around. Every mechanical thing in the house has broken. The furnace shit the bed. My computer is diseased. The car needs ball joints. And yesterday I put metal in the microwave and it blew up."

"Quit putting metal in the microwave," Anna said.

"Just be careful," June said. "I don't want to see you get hurt."

Anna loves June and she's thinking of her now as she zips up her coat. She's wishing for June a streak of good luck, because June deserves it.

David hangs back to check the answering machine while Anna goes outside with Traven. He's relieved that the voice on the machine is Dawn. Her old car has held up and she's made it to the high school reunion four hours away. She'll spend the night in the hotel. That she ends her message with *love you* doesn't register in David's conscience until he catches sight of Anna through the window. She has moved to the center of the driveway and lifted her face to the sun. Her hair is long, a waterfall of wine-brown curling in the light. Eyes closed, she seems to be absorbing the warmth. She reminds him of an exotic plant, which seems apropos since she is a botanist.

When they knew each other before, when he was her teacher, she was unsure of the graduate program she'd chosen. She liked to write and she liked literature, which is how she happened into his class (her legs crossed, leaning forward, blouse open at the collar), but it was a mistake. Her love was plants, after all. He reaches back through time and imagines unbuttoning her blouse. And after all, she is here.

So, when Dawn's voice on the tape, tender and familiar, pronounces her love at the very same time Anna—woman of long-ago dreams—holds her face to the sky, a cold ice drains down his spine.

Unrequited. This is the word that comes to Anna's mind as she stands in the melting snow-balmy air. Traven bounds past her and she opens her eyes. She's blinded momentarily—a black sun ball imprinted in her vision skims across the snow bank, the yard, her rental car.

"Traven," she whispers. The dog stops and tips his head, ears perked, as if he's trying very hard to understand English. "What am I doing here?"

The name B. Traven, David once explained to her, is a pseudonym for the enigmatic author whose true identity was never quite proven. He might have been a German, though he passed as American. Some theories say he was Ret Marut, a political writer jailed during the Bavarian revolution after the First World War. With a death sentence over his head, he escaped and made his way to Mexico. B. Traven was prolific and well versed in all matters and subjects, including several languages. He never wrote by hand, or signed his name anywhere. He may have been more than one man. On the movie set of *The Treasure of the Sierra Madre*, it was said that he disguised himself as his own agent, Hal Croves. When the rumors started, suggesting Croves might actually be Traven, Croves disappeared. In the author's first novel, *The Death Ship*, a young sailor loses his papers and is smuggled from country to country, where he is told that without papers, he doesn't exist. The death ship, David explained, is an old tug, meant to sink for insurance purposes, and so crewed with anonymous souls. Our sailor boards her.

When he told her, Anna couldn't help but think of the crazy Hale-Bopp tailgaters (passports tucked into their belongings as if they'd planned to enter another country), boarding their own death ship—a death spaceship. Fathomless faith.

David won't tell Anna what happens to our hero, the sailor. He wants her to read the novel. It's a book he's loved since he was a boy.

Disappearance and existence, Anna thinks, is somewhat of a paradox. *I think lov eis all a matter of believing,* David once typed to her. *Who are you?* she wrote back.

Traven stares at her, tips his head, mouth open.

"Come here," Anna says and pats her thigh. Traven bows on his front legs, tail end up—a challenge, a standoff—then springs forward. Anna sidesteps and laughs. She strokes his back. He presses against her legs. He's eager to get on the trail. Come on, come on, come on, he pants. Anna wonders what's keeping David. She wants to be away from the house. It will be better in the woods, more relaxed. There's something bothering her, something that settled into her like a weight: the toys in the room.

Anna might have liked to have another child, but time is running out; she had decided to let the time run out. She thinks she might be happy with a dog. She scolds herself for even the smallest indulgence in the idea of a child. Of little Bop.

What she really wants right now is for David to keep touching her. If he keeps touching her, she'll be able to forget everything else. Forget that they hardly know each other. That there are complications—that never-smooth course of true love. His beard has made her chin rough and itchy. She's in love with his lips. Sweet, rounded-middle upper lip. Lips where words fall out and into her ears. A voice that's deeper than she remembered. A soothing voice and unfaltering; it took her by surprise. She'd half expected him to stutter, what with all the quick e-mail incomplete sentences and misspellings and double-written words. She's clearly at an advantage being able to edit and revise before sending her messages. Or is she? All that rewording for perfection. So many silent typed words have passed between them. Passed through wire, sky, cogwheel, sprocket. Queue, launch, vanish, appear. Oh, but David. His hands, and his kind dark eyes that make her believe, that say that this is something, something special. It is. She's sure of it.

Once, David remembers, when Dawn left for a trip, she'd changed her mind at the last minute and driven back, surprising him with a middle of the night visit. She was horny, she said.

It pains him to think how it would hurt Dawn to discover Anna here. And he loves that little boy. He erases Dawn's message and in a moment of panic thinks he might call her at the hotel, tell her to settle in. Don't get the urge to drive after drinking, he might tell her. Or, don't trust that junk heap of a car. Stay put. And he wants to tell her all this to protect her from all the bad things in the world. She's a good, kind person. She's had an awful time of it. She doesn't deserve any more pain and he swears he won't add to it.

David is paralyzed, staring at the telephone. He thinks he must be the biggest coward in the world. He can't believe he has let Anna come here, yet he's so happy she's here. He can't believe how happy he is. It's funny sounding—the word happy—when he says it out loud to the gargoyle face on his way by.

The lines to be drawn are these: kissing, lots of it. Touching, for sure, but no fucking. They agree to these terms as they wide-walk in their snowshoes. The snow sinks slightly under the webs and Anna looks back to see the oval-grate footprints left behind. Traven, light enough to stay atop the crust, dashes ahead. Anna reaches for David's hand. The trail gets steeper and they breathe heavily. Fucking is too intimate.

"There's got to be a better word for it," David says. "Screw. Getting laid?"

"I don't understand that," Anna says. "Which gender owns the verb? How about intercourse?"

"Sounds like something people should do with walkie-talkies," David says.

There are no good words, no right definitions. They only know that they want to be careful and slow, and there is also the matter of Dawn. *Fucking* seems the sort of intimacy that would be the act of betrayal David doesn't want to commit. *Making love* is the act of intimacy Anna wants only when they have complete autonomy. They both know that they are fooling themselves; lines have already been crossed.

But the view from the top is spectacular! Rolling snowy hills and dark mountains in the distance against a dusky sky. David points out Cascom Mountain—the peak with the fire tower—where his parents' cabin sits, tucked in the valley below.

Traven circles them, then sits on the toe of Anna's snowshoe. She takes off her gloves and runs her fingers into his fur. David takes off one glove and slides his hand under Anna's hair at the back of her neck. When she lets go of Traven and turns to David, he pulls her face to his. She nearly topples, but he holds her up and they kiss.

Only Traven notices the bright object hovering over the fire tower. It rises, then dips low, zooms forward, coming closer, growing larger, like a huge shiny bowl. The fur on Traven's back stands on end. He lifts his nose to the breeze and cocks his head. There's a barrage of noise in his sensitive dog ears. Tones he's heard a thousand times before now make sense. *Traven, what am I doing here?* He looks at Anna who is kissing David. He wants to tell her that now he understands what she asked him before. He thinks he could even answer the question, but suddenly he's overwhelmed with David sounds. They are a like a flood, an orchestra warming up, all jumbled and mismatched, thousands of words that blend into one giant ball of good feeling, of friendship. Traven would die for David; he loves him that much. Then, the object takes an abrupt right turn, zipping away over the horizon, and Traven's newfound words slow, like a ball bumping down steps, one after another until they are gone.

In an hour the sky has darkened and David and Anna are back at the house, clapping their snowshoes free of ice. They look up to see their beloved comet once more.

"A spaceship," David says. "How could they believe it?"

Anna speaks close to his ear, "Perhaps it's no less than believing in belief?"

David unzips Anna's coat and slides his hands inside, around to her bottom, and presses her forward. He finds the hem of her sweater and lifts until his palms are on her back, against warm skin.

"Your hands are cold," she says. She grips his jacket at the shoulders and pulls herself closer as his hands circle over bra hooks and around to ribs. She has dropped one hand to his thigh.

What's inside a kiss—inside the heads of lovers? Do they *think* anything at all as they kiss? Is true love born from words or kisses? Both? Heart and mind. Two different dancers. The romantic and the pragmatic matching steps?

There is more information to consider in our lovers' equation. Anna has accepted a year-long grant to study the park rockcress, a rare white flower, *Arabis vivariensis*, that grows principally in Dinosaur National Monument, Colorado. Whether or not she can spend her vacations with David is unknown. David is tenured, house-settled, and dog-owning. Whether or not he can visit her is questionable. There is no easy future for these two. Do they have it in them to weather these storms? To storm these whethers? Anna's kisses say, yes, yes; it's so rare to find someone at all in the world. She is the romantic. She believes in belief—that love is belief. David would claim to be romantic too, but the fact is, he's quite skeptical that long-distance relationships can work. He's not, however, unwilling to hope, by fission or fate, that some path through all the exploding bombs of the universe will open for them.

There is also the more immediate matter of Dawn and Dillon. Which, in our busy day of hiking and kissing, has grown somewhat problematic. Dillon is lethargic and grumpy. The babysitter is having a difficult time. He's not at all acting himself. When she puts her hand to his forehead, she must mask her alarm. His skin is on fire. He's burning up.

And Dawn, who has just now decided to forgo the rest of the sawdust-tasting turkey dinner put on by the reunion committee, has the uncanny feeling that she should check in with the babysitter, see if all is well.

Frankly, there are other forces astir that may affect the short or long of this love story. A junk-heap car that won't start, for instance, holding back an imminent trajectory. A high school crush, revived during the consolation of a worried mother. And because children are the spirit of innocence . . . a message of relief: the fever has broken.

In the long of it, a professor on spring break may suddenly find himself on board a speeding jet to Colorado. In

Dinosaur a sperm spurred upwards, onwards, inwards, in other words, may begin a happy new life.

Hale-Bopp, hurtling itself across the heavens, tail-heavy with rock and dirt and spaceship, will disappear from the sky in just a few short weeks. What it leaves in its wake is up for interpretation.

But come, it's a chill March evening with miles to go before forever and ever; let's get our lovers into bed.

I Never Will

I WAKE UP in the middle of the night for no reason. Thomas would say it's a sign. It's not anything bad now, but maybe later. Like your mind has gone on ahead, glimpsed what's to come, startled you awake. You think you heard a loud noise, the phone ring. It's late; it can't be good; then there's no ring. It's quiet, but the sound is still in your head. The future is calling the present. You aren't there yet, but get ready.

I wake up in the middle of the night and lie there amazed at the moonlight, how bright it is, shining through Thomas's window, catching on the edges of the thin white curtains, turning them blue. There's the old rocking chair with our clothes thrown over the back of it. Thomas's jeans drape over my jeans, the legs dangling together. It's a simple thing, but it makes me feel as if there's a brook rushing through my heart. Thomas is asleep. He sleeps on his back, arms crossed like he's sizing up a situation, though his eyes are closed, his mouth is a line. Whatever the situation is, it's far away from here, deep inside his dream. He is the quietest sleeper in the world. He barely breathes. I put my hand above his nose to feel the air coming out. It does; feathers on my palm, between my fingers. I close my fingers. Open them.

Careful on the creaky floorboards, I pass the rocking chair and stand at the window. Outside the crickets chafe, scratching like a needle run to the end of a record. They stop and start as if questioning my presence. *You can't really be. Here. You can't really. Be here.*

I am here. The birches throw long, hard-edged shadows across the yard in the moonlight. You can see everything, and everything is blue. Papery blue birch bark. I stand at the window. There is the moon, and there is Thomas. He's part Vietnamese, adopted when he was a baby. He doesn't want to know anything more about where he came from. He says he's content with where he is now. Love, he used to say before we were married, is a memory waiting to kill you. I waited a long time for him. I crouched upstream, patient as a bear, while he struggled against the current, flinging himself over rocks and into pools, tugged down and back, drifting, flying forward again.

His hair is like ink in water, seeping across the white pillow. Moths hover wildly in the air, confused by the moonlight. Thomas's eyelids are little crescents, miniature canoes. I feel the weight of the moon—so heavy, sagging in a black hammock. It feels ready to come down. I don't want to remember the future. I don't want it here.

There's no breeze, yet the wind chimes on Thomas's porch ring like ice in a glass. Thomas's yellow dog is on the porch. He raises his head when I come out. I hold the screen door and fit it against the latch behind me so it won't clunk. The dog wags his tail, thumping the couch. *Is it time to get up?* he asks. *No,* I say. *Go back to sleep, Luke.* I smooth his head, hold one furry, thin, cabbage-leaf ear and let it slip from my fingers.

He snorts and flops his head down again. I envy Luke. He is a dog, in a dog's world. He likes canned food, and he loves to lick our plates.

I could stay out here all night in the balmy air. The air smells of salt marsh, blown in from the coast, and cut grass, and a little sweetness from the pines behind the house. I could stay right here in this moment forever. I walk around the porch to Thomas's window and look in on him. I'm a ghost. I'm a mysterious woman out in the night with long yellow hair and Thomas's big T-shirt that grazes my thighs. I could take it off and be naked on the porch in the moonlight, out here in the country, in the private night.

I am naked. I am outside Thomas's window. He's asleep on his back. He looks like he's sizing up a situation. He has a bold, forward-jutting chin, tapering from wide cheek bones. His face is curved like an instrument. I could strum his temples, play his mouth. Luke watches me as I leave the porch and stand in the middle of the yard. He wags his tail, once, twice, and stays on his couch, sunk into the hollow of his cushion. My skin is shaded blue and blue-gray and blue-white in the moonlight. Never make wishes on the moon; it's bad luck. I don't speak to it, but I want to. It's hard not to. I am blue, and I am naked. I wish Thomas were dancing with me.

Thomas is dancing with me. His hair is loose and long. He lifts his knees high. He curves his arms to the space around me, but he doesn't touch me. He shapes the air around me, following my outline. We laugh—silly, crazy people, in the middle of the night, under the moon. Luke edges off the couch, takes the stairs slowly, painfully, until he's in the grass too. *Here boy, if you must join us.* We pat him for his efforts, and press our faces into his tattered dog fur. He smells like road dust and worn hide. Thomas and I weave and lean to invisible music.

Thomas plays his guitar. He sits on the porch couch, sunk in the cushions, leg over knee, plucking the strings. Luke lies at his feet, head resting on the floor, eyes raised, skeptical. Thomas begins to hum low, staggered, stop and start. He is writing a song for me. He hasn't got the lyrics yet, just the melody. Luke flops onto his side, sleeps. The light in the kitchen is amber, like netting, falling over our long wooden table. There are golden apples in a bowl. I am inside, while Thomas is outside on the porch working on his song. I'm in charge of the salad, so I'm cutting vegetables. Yellow peppers, red peppers, green peppers. With a fork, I serrate the skin of a cucumber. I rub smooth, white-tan mushrooms with my thumb under ice cold water, then slice them thin. I hear Thomas's fingers slide over the strings, bend the notes. My fingers are numb. He's humming, then there are a few words that dissolve, melt away to melody. Then strumming. Shivers rattle through me.

I wake up in the middle of the night, and I remember all the things to come. But not here. Not now.

Thomas cooks me his special casserole, which has a name. It's *Kate's Casserole That Kate Loves the Best.* Especially with the bread crumbs on top that get crunchy with cheese. Thomas makes this dish, and I make the salad. We drink cool white wine and sit under warm yellow light, eat. Then we give Luke the plates to clean. Thomas looks around the kitchen, leans back in his chair. "Here's a moment," he says, and I know he means it was worth getting here. Worth the risk. Later we gather the dishes off the floor and pile them in the sink for tomorrow. Thomas plays me the melody of the song. His voice is a rill around a rock, a swirl.

We sit on the porch steps and look at the moon. Luke sleeps behind us on the couch. I push my hands under Thomas's shirt, circle his nipples with my fingers. He breathes a note, then a hum below the note. Later when we are sleeping, cells begin to divide inside me.

The future is calling for me again. Patient bear. I waited a long time for Thomas. He's a difficult man. Stubborn. Sometimes he can't speak. Thoughts collide with language. Fear eats his words. I used to get mad at him. *How can you be afraid of love? Of me?* Now I know. I know exactly. Cruel moon. I don't want to remember very far ahead. I don't want to go past our son.

Sun. I love Thomas's legs in his straight-leg jeans. The cuffs bunch a little around his cowboy boots. Thomas looks like a cowboy in his brimmed, ragged hat. He sings old country songs, strolling across the lawn with his Gibson, the strap over his shoulder. He holds the guitar, lifting the neck, strumming, lifting it up and down as if he's waltzing with it. He has those long legs and those boots. He wears the T-shirt I sometimes wear to bed. The collar is large, stretched out. His skin is soft brown, the color of the underside of mushrooms. He struts to the edge of the yard, strumming chords, singing to the hay field, the Maine sky, the world out there beyond us. His voice is clear, full of spirit. His shoulders, the strap across his back, the muscle in his arm. Fingertips press notes, drawing music from metal wound around itself, strings across the sound hole, vibrating inside the hollow. From that comes this. Music. Look at him. Grass on the toes of his boots. That silly hat. Those faded jeans. I could look at his sweet ass all day for the rest of my life.

Luke howls if you get him going. He howls in tune to "Crazy." He has a part and he knows it well. I love the way Luke loves Thomas. Look at Luke sitting on the front seat of Thomas's truck—all day sometimes—just in case Thomas might be going somewhere. They drive off, Luke in the passenger seat, like some old prow-headed fellow, Thomas's pal. The truck rumbles away, kicking up dust. Tools and cans of nails, jangling in the bed.

Thomas wakes up in the night for no reason and goes out to sit with Luke. I roll over and there's just blue moonlight all across the white sheets, rippling with the folds. A worry rises—a high note left in the air, reminding me to get ready.

You can't describe music, so let me tell you about the moon. It hangs at a tilt, face turned aside, scanning the situation, the earth, the field over there on the far side of our land. The full moonlight is as bright as day, only not quite. It covers the lawn, the porch steps, the floor, the field out there. The bowl of golden apples, turned blue. Wide boards that creak in some places. When we make dinner we sometimes get to making music with the floorboards. We can creak-step the refrain of "The Brand New Tennessee Waltz." We can step out the first long notes of "Crazy." And Luke howls.

I swear, I never asked the moon for anything.

ooooooooo

Thomas writes like crazy, full of ideas. He has the melody, but the lyrics are difficult. A man sees a woman outside the window. She reaches up, sifts her fingers through the wind chimes. It's a simple thing. The man tries to resist his heart. Only a few words: *If I don't leave now . . .*

I stand outside his window. He wakes up for no reason.

"Kate?" he says, so calm. "That you out there?"

"No," I say. "It's not me."

"Did you turn on the moon?"

"Too bright?"

"I'm sleepy, Katybug. Come back to bed."

In bed Thomas pulls me on top of him. He shrugs the T-shirt up and puts his hands on my waist. He tilts me down so he can put his mouth on my mouth, then my nipple. His teeth pinch, and I sink into him. I'll feel it tomorrow—the echo of it—a memory that still makes my skin respond: a blast of sand-full wind, hot and prickling, then cooling. He was there, touching me.

We live way out. Sometimes gulls come inland—white bows pinned in the blue, riding the currents. There's a dirt road that cuts through hay fields. You can hear a truck coming for a long way, grinding over the gravel, turning where our road comes off River Road, toolbox banging when the tires hit bumps. Flocks of black birds rise out of the fields, and fall like veils. You can hear things going away a long ways, too.

My stomach is as big as the moon. I dance in the kitchen, rock and roll. My body doesn't fit between the counter and the table. I rest my belly on the table. Here, baby, take a load off.

I bring Luke the plates and hold them for him so he doesn't have to get off the couch. His tongue twists across the plate, lapping it up. His tail bobs once, twice when he hears "Crazy" on the floorboards. He lifts his head, cloudy eyes, and makes a whimpering note, long and descending, no longer a howl. Thomas can barely stand it. He doesn't think we should put the idea in Luke's head anymore.

Thomas sucks my nipples to make them tough for the baby. He presses his ear to my belly, listens, and rests his palms in different places, finding the head, the knees.

At night I wake up when the baby kicks. That's the reason. I lie on my side next to Thomas. "This baby will be a great drummer," he says.

Thomas searches everywhere, but Luke is gone. Only yellow-gray hairs on the cushions, like dried milkweed fluff. Thomas squats next to the couch and holds his head. He puts his palms in the hollow Luke left behind. He rocks on the heels of his cowboy boots. I stroke his hair and put my hand on the back of his neck, rub with my thumb. Thomas bats my hand away. I try again. He grips my wrist hard, presses my hand against my thigh, shoves, and lets go.

I play Mozart on the old record player for the baby. The sun glints on the notes, like prisms throwing rainbows up the walls, across glass and furniture. Shimmering, droplets hitting a hot surface, bouncing everywhere. We are going to have a boy. They showed us photographs. The head, the foot. A little boy that we'll name Tommy. Little T. The photo is black and white. We stare at the ghost lines making translucent shapes.

Little fish.

Thomas and I go down to the brook and cross out to the big, smooth rock. The rock is shaped like a wide rowboat. We lie in the sun with the brook roaring and spilling and foaming around rocks and heading fast downstream where it cuts below our road, under the bridge. Thomas falls asleep. I check his breath.

We breathe. Thomas and I, and then the baby. Our little T. Eyelids as smooth as beach pebbles. Little crescents. We lie with him between us, and feel our hearts filling up, so big, overflowing, water everywhere, creeping across the floor, filling the cracks between the boards. The furniture bobs, the rocking chair rocks. Luke's old tin bowl floats away, gone forever. The house drifts, sways gently. We sing and play music, strum guitar. Thomas writes new melodies. We sing old country songs and Little T makes a round *oh* mouth, a nipple-hunting mouth, then later a smile mouth. It is our own smile coming back to us. His little fingers are strong. He howls. The chimes tinkle. Sometimes we think we hear Luke, his tail thumping against the couch cushions.

We owe everybody money. Thomas refuses to pay the mechanic for the engine work because he says the bill is too high. "Pay half," I say. "Some. He *did* fix it when no one else could." Thomas kicks the kitchen chair out of his way, slams the door. Cigarette smoke trails in through the screens. I hate the smell. "I hate that!" I say to the sink full of dishes. To the chair on its back, to Thomas out there in the yard. We owe our neighbor for four cords of firewood, too, but Thomas can probably trade for carpentry work. If he will; if he doesn't stay mad about so much poplar mixed in with the other hardwoods.

ooooooooooo

I wake up in the middle of the night. Thomas has no language when it comes to what he feels. I used to say, *How can you be afraid of love?* That was before I knew the answer. Before our son.

Little T loves high places. He dreams that he can fly. He wants a puppy. We are three. We are black-haired, blond, Vietnamese, Norwegian, notes upon notes. *I could see the roof down there, Mommy, and the truck and there was a butterfly inside me, like going high on a swing.*

He loves music. We grow up and dance. We show T how to make the floor creak. He teaches us "Twinkle Twinkle." It's as if he is water flowing through us. From us. From our feet. Little star. We join the world by the hands and follow: nursery school, playmates, other parents, *Sesame Street.* The shelves fill up with books about bears, dogs, and airplanes. *Mary Poppins* stays in the VCR. I make up a story about a boy who can fly and he has me tell it over and over. We learn to love the Beatles again—the only music allowed in the truck while traveling with Master T. I work at a newspaper part-time and start school again, one class at a time. Thomas takes on more jobs—boats and houses. T grows to be four years old. Four years is a tiny drop. A grace note. Here it is again. Sandpaper scuff. A sneaker on roof shingles. I don't want to look up. I don't want to look up.

At the funeral Thomas's eyes are slivers of ice that won't shift from the horizon. His blood moans as it freezes. The grave is so small. My knees go. The ground comes up to meet me.

ooooooooo

Start at the beginning, like a record—put the needle back, play the song again and again, catch it before it moves on to the next band. Stay here. Stay in the part before and never arrive at the part after. Hold the refrain. Don't finish the song. Go back. Quick. Cucumbers. The moonlight. Luke's tail thumping on the couch. Before that: The first time I saw Thomas's land. His small white house, sitting at the edge of a field, pine trees towering over the roof behind it. His hand on my leg in the truck, stones chattering under the tires. His crescent eyes, full of light and sparkle. Turn on the radio. *Crazy, I'm crazy for loving.* The toe of his boot on the gas pedal. The house growing larger. The hole in his jeans, mushroom-tan knee showing through. A simple thing. *It scares me, Kate.* Turn off River Road, tires skittering. *How much I want you.* Clouds of yellow dust hover above the road a long ways behind us. I am here. I want to. Stay here. Let me stay.

Sun in my eyes. A shape on the peak of the roof. A giant bird? T with an umbrella. One foot on, one foot off. Then flying. Then falling. My arms reaching, my body trying to get there in time. Not in time. Never in time.

I wake up in the middle of the night and reach for Thomas, but he isn't there.

He isn't here. The crickets chafe. *T's T's Tsdead Tsdead.*
Moonlight spills over the windowsill.
Chimes ring, though it's incredibly still.
If I don't leave now, I never will.

A Story About a Boat That Came Out of the Night

DAVID LAY AWAKE LISTENING to the tapping of the typewriter in the next room. It was his father, up late working. Earlier in the night it had been raining. Sometimes the typewriter sounded like rain on the roof and David would have to remind himself it was not rain but the tap of the keys printing out words. It was a soothing sound, really, much like rain, its beat consistent if not repetitive even in its random nature.

It was dark in the room. Katy slept below him on the lower bunk. She made no sound at all as she slept. It occurred to him that if he didn't know better, he would think he was alone in the room. He shut his eyes and looked at the darkness on the inside of his eyelids. Sometimes it seemed he saw things there—small light-colored shapes floating like dust particles or pond water organisms. But then, swept up in his thoughts, he would lose hold of his concentration and realize that he was not seeing anything at all but only thinking, as if his eyes had turned around to watch a movie in his brain.

Tap, tap, tap. He counted the taps. They came in fives and sevens. Sometimes fours and twos. Katy was eight. He was ten. Back home he had his own room, but here, in the summers, he and Katy shared a room. He had the top bunk. She had the bottom bunk.

Someday, his father told him, they would add onto the cabin and they'd each have their own rooms. His father and mother shared a room for sleeping but there was the other room for his father: the writing room. It was small, more like a closet, and would someday be a bathroom. Here, at the cabin, they had an outhouse across the yard in the woods.

The tapping stopped. Maybe his father was done for the night and now he'd come get them. Then there was more tapping and then it stopped again. Maybe he was just thinking. But soon, soon he'd be done and he'd come wake them and take them to Cascom Lake where they'd fish for horned pout.

David made a picture of his father in the room. It was dark all around the edges. The stones rising to the windowsills and the logs going up from there would be in shadow because right in the middle of the room was the desk with the gooseneck lamp on it. The light from the lamp fell over his father's arms and the front of his head. It made the paper in the typewriter seem very white—almost as white as the T-shirt his father wore, only just the front of it because the light didn't reach around over his shoulders and back. On the paper were the tiny shapes of black letters, their lines as fine as the legs of ants. The letters made words, David knew, but he didn't yet know what the story was all about. It was a novel. His father was a writer. In the story there was something about a man who rode a motorcycle; that was part of it.

His father wanted to buy a Honda. David had heard talk of this between his father and mother. A real motorcycle, not like the blue Vespa scooter his father had now. It would be better than the Vespa. It would be faster. His father told him that

Vespa was the word for wasp. The Honda wouldn't be slow and heavy like a wasp; it would be quick and dangerous like a yellow jacket. David's mother was worried about the motorcycle.

Sometimes his father took him for rides on the Vespa. He would wear Katy's black velvet-covered horseback riding helmet. It was tight and the elastic strap dug in under his chin, but he had to wear a hardhat if he was going to ride on the scooter.

On the Vespa he put his arms around his father's waist and laced his fingers together. Sometimes when they went around corners and the scooter angled over, tipping low into the turn, the pavement coming up close and shooting by like fast water, his father would let go of one handlebar to touch the tops of David's fingers. His father wore gloves and David felt the leather against his fingers as cool and sticky as the underside of a turtle.

Someday he and his father would ride motorcycles through the night. They would wear white helmets. They would look like two full moons chasing each other through the trees.

"What's the story about?" David asked his father. It was dark and still on the lake. Katy had fallen asleep in the bow up under the thwarts. The canoe drifted over the black water. Sometimes his father would slide one of the paddles out and fan it through the water, moving the canoe back out from the shore away from the eerie stumps and fallen trees that came up in the darkness, showing in the Coleman lantern. David didn't like to look at the things in the water but this was where the fish were. They had caught several, which were now in the bucket, their dangerous whiskers folded back on each other. Katy hadn't caught any before she crawled into her nest of jackets and fell asleep. Usually she didn't come with them.

Their mother thought Katy was too young to go out in the boat at night, but sometimes Katy got her way. Katy didn't like to fish so much as she liked to listen to the water moving under the floor of the canoe.

"Now that's a hard question to answer," his father said. He turned a bit on his seat. They mostly sat with their backs to each other, their lines on opposite sides of the canoe. The smoke from his father's pipe drifted by. It was dry and good like the smell of birch bark starting up a fire.

"I suppose I'm not really sure," he said. "It's about all sorts of things—life. A story is more than just what happens in it. The story is under and between what happens."

"But what happens?"

"Lots of things happen. It's about some people and some troubles they go through. You'll see. You can read it when it's done."

"Oh," David said. He tugged his pole up a little and waited to see if his father might say something else, but he didn't for a long while.

Out in the dark there were stars, sometimes hidden by the leaves and branches of trees that hung out over the water. There were peepers churning out their sound from the banks and the occasional lapping, dribbling sound of water against the aluminum canoe like gentle hands trying to hold water up to a mouth.

Off in the distance they heard the motor. At first they didn't see its light, then it appeared from around the cove, moving through the darkness. They both watched it, a yellow light unattached to anything in the dark, turning now and heading toward shore, toward them, it seemed, although it was hard to tell because the world was so black with no edges or boundaries to set against its progress. Its engine, as smooth as a motorcycle on a clear stretch of road, hummed evenly.

They watched as the light came closer, now headed in their direction. His father shifted a little, redirecting his pole. David didn't move, waiting for the thing to pass as one might wait for an airplane to pass over before finishing a sentence. It moved closer. He could just make out the line of the bow. It was a large motorboat moving fast enough to tip its front up out of the water.

"Jesus," his father said. "They must see our light." He pulled his pole back so its butt rested on the bottom of the boat, the line still out in the water.

"Goddamn," his father said, standing, his legs bent and wide apart to keep balance. He reached back, hooked his fingers into the bail of the lantern and lifted it. He held it up and swung it back and forth. The boat kept coming, faster now, and louder.

David dropped his pole into the canoe and grabbed hold of the gunwales on either side. It was going to run right into them! His foot kicked out, scraping across the bottom of the boat and into where Katy slept, hitting her leg or foot. His father was yelling, waving the lantern and his arms.

David yelled too, "We're here. Stop!" but the boat came on and then spun sideways, veering off a few yards from them. Almost immediately the canoe was hit by the wake, lifted and rolled.

David saw his father going backwards in a wash of light from the lantern, and then there was silence. David was under water. It felt cold and his arms were heavy. The canoe had slammed against him and there was a pain in his shoulder as he moved his arms, pulling for the surface. His life jacket lifted around his neck, snug against his chin. Something caught against his hands, cloth or a jacket, and he pushed it down with the movement of his stroke. When he came up he heard his father yelling.

"Dad!" David called out, but water was in his mouth and the word didn't come out right.

"David! Kate!" his father yelled.

"Dad!"

"Where's Kate? Where's Kate?"

David moved his arms, keeping his head above the surface. The water was dark. He thought he saw the canoe lolling upside down a few yards away. He began to swim toward it but then he wasn't sure if it was the canoe or a stump. He didn't want to go near the stumps. But he should. He should grab hold of something.

"Kate!" His father was behind the canoe. David put his hands on it and it rolled a little. He saw his father's arm come up on top of it and the whole thing rolled over right side up, only submerged in the water.

"Stay with the canoe," he said. "Oh, dear God, where's Kate?" His father's words were deep in his throat.

"Kate!" David yelled. He wanted to help. His legs felt heavy and slow in the water as he moved them back and forth. The water was deep, his feet didn't reach bottom, didn't touch or brush against anything down there in the darkness below.

There was a stillness for a moment. The only sounds were the peepers and the ones he or his father made moving their arms or legs through the water. David held on to the canoe. It floated just at the surface of the water. The motorboat was gone. There was no sound of its engine. And then they heard her crying. At first David thought it was the peepers, but then her noise sounded like words and she was bawling and speaking at the same time.

"Katy, where are you? Oh, Jesus, thank God! Hold tight, Katybug." His father moved away from the canoe, swimming into the dark.

She had got herself up on one of the stumps close to the shore. His father picked her off and swam her in, then came back for David. They swam on either side of the canoe, dragging it along, maneuvering through swamped trees until their feet touched bottom and they stood to walk through the water the rest of the way. Katy sat huddled on the bank.

"What in the hell could have been in those people's minds?" David's mother said. David sat next to his father on the couch. Katy, wrapped in a blanket in her mother's lap, turned herself as if she were trying to hide her face under her mother's arm. They had washed and changed into dry clothes. They had a fire going hot.

"You could have drowned," his mother said. Water came up in her eyes.

"We're okay, Carey," his father said. "Everything's okay now. No matter what happened, we're okay. It happened. It's over."

"There's just no sense in it," she said. "They must have seen you. They must have realized they swamped you."

David looked at his father to see what he would say but he didn't say anything, just stared toward the fire. The light from the fireplace moved shadows around the room and wavered across his father's face. David felt the heat on his knees and feet. He saw Katy and his mother in the reflection on the window, backed by the darkness outside, across the room. He saw his father's hand lying next to his leg on the couch. David reached out and put his fingers on top of his father's fingers. He sensed his father turning to look at him, but he didn't want to look up; he wanted to keep his eyes on their hands.

After a moment his father took a deep breath sucking in air as if he were going to say something, but he didn't; the air came out again and then his father's fingers splayed apart a little and let David's fingers fall between them.

The next day they went back to Cascom Lake—just David and his father. Katy stayed home with their mother.

It didn't look the same as in the dark. The bank where they'd pulled the canoe out seemed less steep. There were footprints there—big ones from his father's boots and smaller ones from David's sneakers. The treads, skeleton-like imprints sunk into the mud, looked like the rounded shells of ancient trilobites. In some places there were bare footprints where Katy's toes made little round pods.

One of the paddles floated near the bank a few yards away. His father went to retrieve it. David scanned the water. It was smooth and gray. The sky was gray too. Water reflects the sky. The stumps reflected in the water too, sending wavering shadows—thin and dark over the water.

It was probably there, between the big one and the one whose roots showed underneath it like a hand with its fingers reaching down under the water as if it were going to pick something up, pinch something up—it was probably near there that they capsized.

Maybe the bucket was down there, and the tarp, Katy's missing sneaker, and the Coleman lantern. His father would wade out and look. David would walk the bank, maybe all the way around the corner, past the thicket of trees. He'd keep his eyes peeled for the other paddle.

Out on the lake there were motorboats, their chainsaw motors buzzing sometimes loud, and then soft, in the distance. The water lapped up along the shore, just nudging it gently, making little sounds—sounds like swallowing with a dry throat or maybe like when you taste something unfamiliar.

He walked all the way around the little point of land that jutted out—the peninsula, where the trees grew sparse and the ground gave way to granite ledge, sliding smooth and gray into the water. The lake was rougher here on this side. White caps, as slender and fast as the fingery wings of birds, spread then folded, disappearing in the roll of the waves.

"David!" It was his father calling. He wished he'd found the paddle, but he hadn't. He hurried back along the bank. Maybe the paddle was down the other way.

"David!"

"Here I am," David said. Bushes scraped across his legs.

"Let's go," his father said. There was the bucket, and the tarp, wet and dirty, lay on the bank. "I can't find anything else. It's dark down there, mucky."

"I couldn't find the paddle," David said.

"It could be anywhere. Maybe it'll turn up. Someone will turn it in," his father said.

If someone found the paddle, they might think a boat had sunk. Maybe they'd think some people drowned. But that's not what happened. They didn't drown—nobody did.

After, they drove on the road around the lake toward the marina.

"I want to report what happened," his father said. "Maybe they'll know something."

"How will they know?"

"I don't know. They probably won't, but you never know. They might have an idea."

"If they know, what will happen?"

"I don't know. Probably nothing will happen."

"Nothing?"

"Probably not." His father's hands were tight on the steering wheel. His knuckles were white. "Those bastards," his father said suddenly. "They don't even know what they did!"

David looked at his father. His lips were pressed tight. After a while, he took one hand off the steering wheel and curled it around the ball of the stick shift. He didn't change gears, though, just let his hand rest there. Then he said, "I'm glad you were with me, David. I was real glad to have you with me last night. You did everything just right."

David was way down under. It was heavy and dark. There was a water sound in his ears, thick and muffled. He saw the water lapping around a stump. It made a funny tick, tick sound as it came between and up under the exposed roots. And then, he was coming up. He felt his life jacket pulling around his face. It was dark and then when he broke through the surface, he felt heavy as if he'd been asleep for a very long time. It was two days ago that they'd gone over in the canoe. The paddle still hadn't turned up.

It was dark in the room except for a thin spray of light that came in under the door. There was the tapping sound. His father was up late working, writing into the night. Maybe he would finish the story tonight. Maybe the man on the motorcycle would get to wherever he was going and his father would end the novel. He'd write "The End" and it would be done and then they could build a bathroom and other rooms so he and Katy could have their own. And when it was done, his father would buy a Honda.

And then his father would start another book because that's what he did. When this one was done, he'd write another one.

Maybe sometime his father would write about the boat that came out of the night. Or maybe David could write that story himself. If he did, it would be about more than just that. It would be about all sorts of things. Oh yes, it would be much more than that.

Cold-Fire: Epilogue

THE FLAT WHERE I LIVE, the second floor of a three-story Victorian, is in Kittery, Maine, just across the New Hampshire border. You can see the bay from the kitchen window. White-caps, pinched up by a sharp wind, shred the surface of the harbor, and fat tugboats, roped together by the pier, rock on the swells, wait for ships. Farther away, the Piscataqua Bridge makes a horseshoe over the river—army green metal against a stark sky. It could snow.

At this distance, everything—the cars going back and forth across the bridge, the wind, thrashing the water—is soundless. The only noise is from the family living upstairs. Their voices come through the ceiling muted, words inaudible.

This morning I closed the cabin for winter: drained the water tank, pulled the circuit breaker, secured the doors. I turned my back to the mountain and walked away. It watched me leave; I felt it. In my car, I rumbled down Cascom Mountain Road, crossed the old wooden bridge, hardly a glance at the shallow brook below, and into Leah where I stopped for gas. In another half hour, I hit Route 93 South. In Concord, it spit snow as I turned east toward the coast. Three hours later, I am here.

It was chilly in these rooms when I first came in, but now the thermostat is up all the way; the radiator ticks. The kettle is on for tea.

The mailbox was jammed with junk, but I know as I'm sorting through it that I'm hoping for a letter from Thomas. And behold! Here it is. All the way from Vietnam, where Thomas has been for the last four months. This time there's a photograph of a dark-haired Asian boy. Thomas's half nephew. The boy is playing a guitar that is too large for him, reaching around it with his little arms. He seems to be singing, mouth in an O, eyes squinting with concentration. Next to the boy, looking on with a half smile, is a young woman—the boy's mother, I presume.

On the back of the photograph, Thomas has written: *Teaching Li to play like Mississippi John Hurt.* I can imagine Thomas grinning, knowing that John Hurt is my favorite: *I got a mother in Beulah Land . . .*

It occurs to me that Thomas didn't outrun grief, but rather, he followed it, let it lead him to his past, to his mother's country, where now he's teaching little boys to play guitar and sing songs. He's come a long way.

The salutation at the end of his letter is written in Vietnamese—words I can't translate, but don't need to. They are in the place where you would send your love. Below that: *Arrive Boston, November 15th.* The meaning here is harder to read, but my eyes spark and go bleary.

In the photograph, the boy's mother reaches out, arms crooked in such a way that suggests she wants to help her son hang onto the big guitar, but she's holding back, allowing him to do it on his own.

Before I know it, I have made my way to the bedroom. What I'm looking for is on the shelf in the back of the closet, under a pile of blankets. In one furious motion I have the umbrella in my grip, take it to the kitchen, and lay it on the table. The kettle screams. I quiet it, pour a mug, sit.

Here it is—from curved handle to silver tip; black nylon, spiraled and crimped together by its tie and snap. No evidence of the broken spokes inside. I touch it lightly, two quick pats, then rest my whole hand on top of it. So daring, our little aeronaut.

The children are laughing up there. They sound like geese. Far off, migrating geese—aching throats, communicating with each other as they must make that brave, headlong flight to the other home.

Publication Credits

GRATEFUL ACKNOWLEDGMENT is made to the following journals where some of these stories, in slightly different form, first appeared:

"Cold-Fire": *The Iowa Review*

"Before This Day There Were Many Days": *Ploughshares*

"The Woman in the Woods": *Story*

"Wishbones": *The Missouri Review*

"The Last Thing I Remember": *Third Coast*

"Jupiter Shining, North of the Moon": *The Northwest Review*

"The Man from Nothing": *Whetstone*

"The Matter of Dawn": *Willow Springs*

"A Story About a Boat That Came Out of the Night": *The North American Review*

Photo: Liz Williams

Ann Joslin Williams holds degrees from the University of New Hampshire and from the Iowa Writers' Workshop, where she was a Teaching Writing Fellow. She is also the recipient of fellowships from Stanford University's Wallace Stegner Program and from the Vermont Studio Center. Her work has appeared in many journals, including *The Iowa Review*, *The Missouri Review*, *StoryQuarterly*, and *Ploughshares*, and was cited in *Best American Short Stories, 2002*. She lives in San Francisco and teaches at the California College of the Arts.